BORIS KRIGER

ALPHA and OMEGA

AN UNFORGETTABLE STORY OF UNCONDITIONAL LOVE

Editor *Valentina Kizilo*

We frequently commit rash acts, whose prices in the course of time become dear, that gnaw at the soft bases of our hearts. And who knows, if in reality we are at fault, or is it some God trade who imposes his will upon us so that we are doomed to repeated adversity? Beset by death, by unhappy love, by betrayal… Alpha and Omega is a novel about *unconditional* love, which is the only form of love that in all fairness can be called love. Love not for something and not in spite of something. Love, as the main concern, becoming the core of life, the beginning and end, the alpha and omega…

ISBN: 978-1-105-68739-6

Published in Canada by Altaspera Publishing & Literary Agency Inc.

α

The ABC's of life – anything but simple. It is written in intricate characters, but in their understanding is hidden great happiness.

In one early Christian manuscript missing in other sources, Christ's words are manifested. When he was asked if it were possible to sometimes break a commandment, the Messiah answered, "Blessed are they who know what they are doing;" and then he pondered and added, "Cursed are those who do not know."

Meandering in the midst of the alphabet soup of one's own life, it is difficult to find the beginning and the end, the alpha and omega, which guides one through life. Alas, this alphabet is not taught in a single school in the world.

…The lecture dragged on endlessly, like the gray monotony of a pedestrian underpass.

"There is nothing like… the Philosophy Department…" Nikolai griped to himself. He already tried everything to relieve his boredom, with the exception of mischief that would get him thrown out the door: he gazed in all directions, wrote notes to the two girls sitting next to him, and thumbed through his textbook… The bald professor droned on and on, monotonously making a point to himself, and in a voice that could inflame one's brain and set it on end. "What rubbish", wrote Nikolai on wrinkled bit of paper which he pass on to his neighbor. She sat so closely to him that he had not yet managed to look her over. He only smelled the light scent of her fragrance, fresh and unobtrusive. A peripheral glance gave him the sense of something extremely agreeable, dressed in a lilac outfit. But, do not turn and stare at her! With this in mind, he looked everywhere but in that direction, waiting till the end of the lecture so that he could make the full visual acquaintance of his neighbor, his partner in witty correspondence. He heard a muted giggle. The girl had read his note. He wanted to write something more, but their bonds had been released – the lecture was over.

Nikolai got up and nonchalantly glanced at his neighbor: two ocean blue eyes returned his gaze so brightly and cheerfully, that he could not tear his eyes away from hers. The girl noted his perplexity and smiled.

"There are times when first meeting someone that life becomes a truly entertaining process," he thought and shifted his glance. A strange feeling of light gladness surrounded him. He was roused to inspiration. He still wished, as he did before, to look over the girl, in detail, to coolly and thoroughly evaluate her height and her shape, to find shortcomings so as to put his mind at rest so that it would not be such a great loss if he didn't win her... But right now it was completely impossible, definitely not convenient, so therefore it was necessary to put aside this plan for a better moment.

"I am Mira," the girl presented herself somewhat cheerfully.

"From which star?" he clumsily joked.

"From the very same," she laughed. "You don't get it; I am Russian, and my name is such because my father is turned on about world peace.

"Nikolai," he awkwardly confided. He did not like his name. "Only not for the last tsar," he implored.

"How did you guess that I was about to say that?"

"Unfortunately, we are all rather the same... And there is nothing you can do about it. Stamped out like sheets of copy paper!" Nikolai said out of the blue, surprising even himself; and he immediately regretted it. Why did he say that? Would it suddenly offend her?

But Mira responded by suddenly stepping back and displaying herself, raising her arms up and lightly posturing her body and legs. And there was nothing he could do but stare at her... She was ravishing; a cute sweater covered her enchanting swells, and her jeans emphasized the curve of her thighs. He was even bold enough to stare down her legs. He loved to secretly study women's feet, and even though it seemed indecent to him, he could not but take the liberty of doing so. Neat gray sneakers rounded off the girl's outfit.

"And do you still insist that we are all of the same mold?" asked Mira as she daringly glanced at him up and at down, stopping indecently at a suggestive area. He could feel himself reddening.

Seeing that she had rattled her companion, she also blushed and glanced away.

They left the student building and leisurely strolled in the direction of the train to Vasilievsky island. Nikolai thought that he should ask to carry her bag, but it did not appear to be that heavy, and he changed his mind.

"Do you go to classes without notebooks?"

"I just have one for all my classes…"

"That's original…"

"It's convenient; I never mix up which one I need to bring on any given day…"

He intently rifled through the pages.

"What great weather!" she said. "I love Fall…"

"Me too…"

"Look at those clouds!"

"Atmospheric phenomena," he retorted. "People assign too much meaning to clouds. They look at them and admire them. But in fact its all just water vapor," he chimed his favorite tune.

"A philosopher! Are you going for nihilism as well? Nowadays that's considered quite old-fashioned… But generally you are quite young after all."

"And you're an oldie?"

"What do you think?"

"It seems to me, wait… let me think. I think you should be about seventeen. You went to college right after high-school, right?

"Ha! No… I'm twenty-one, married, with a one-year old son…"

"Not possible!"

"How old are you?"

"Eighteen"

"Well, so you see, I'm older than you.

"And you have already outgrown nihilism, Nietzsche, Chopin… well, how do I say it.. Schopenhauer?"

"I've done all, even Chopin…"

"And I, it seems, still haven't… You know, I thought that I was not susceptible to any influence. Nobody's… As it happens, if you give nobody authority over your own will, they can still find their way through your unconscious…"

"Yes. Since I am an old woman I know this well."

"I swear I thought you just got out of high-school…"

"So you DO think that I am an old woman?"

"No! Except its too bad that you are…"

"Old?"

"Married…"

"Yes, and I'm sorry. But there's nothing to be done. The bonds of love, faithful marriage, strong ties of family duty…"

"When were you able to do so much?"

"Well, there was enough time… Now girls grow up fast."

"And I, it seems, still have not grown up…"

"So you do not have anyone?"

"No, I'm not an orphan…"

"I understand. One doesn't frequently meet orphans. I meant…"

"A girl? No… I was in love once, but it was childish, and she was really foolish…"

He listened to himself as if from a distance as he marveled that he was so willingly answering such provocative questions.

"Do you mean to say, that you never…" she faltered for a second. "Well, did you ever have anyone?"

"If that's what you mean… then yes, never…"

"No way! You're playing with me."

He again desperately rifled through the pages.

"As you wish… you don't have to believe me."

"You're just pretending to be inexperienced, but, by the looks of it, you're not telling all…"

"That's because I worked as an assistant in a morgue."

"Oh my god! How did you end up there?"

"I don't know… concatenation of circumstances…"

"Then at least the anatomy of the female body won't be a secret to you?

"No… However, I don't want to use the knowledge I gained in the autopsy room…"

"Thanks a lot! You are an interesting young man…"

"And you are an interesting old woman."

"Does that mean you are a neophyte in the game of love?"

"And you aren't a neophyte? Or *neophyta*… How does one say 'neophyte' for a girl?"

"Neophytress…" Mira burst out laughing.

For some reason he was getting peeved.

"You like to play that you're wise with experience. You had you first wedding night only a year-and-a-half ago… Am I wrong?"

"Oh, you'll be the death of me… You spent your best years in a morgue, you're innocent, like an angel…"

"Angels always take care of the dead… That's their work."

"A modern girl usually has her first experience – sometimes at fifteen, and sometimes at thirteen…"

"You should remember, you're talking about yourself…"

"Are you judging me?"

"But, why should I?" he tried to hide his annoyance. "We are all products of our time… And how many have there been?"

"Lovers? You really want to know?"

"I don't know how we got onto this... Let's change topics."

"Fifteen..."

"What – fifteen?"

"Lovers..."

"Including your husband?"

"No."

He fell silent and awkwardly flapped his hand:

"The weather is wonderful... And your clouds are sailing with the wind."

"Did I disappoint you?" she asked tenderly.

"No."

"I can see you are disappointed. You thought I was a naïve schoolgirl..."

"I didn't think anything."

"C'mon, come clean..."

"I wasn't thinking of anything... That is, I thought... But it makes no difference... The world's turned inside-out..."

"The world's always been like that... It only seems that the world is changing. But it really isn't..." she halted and fell silent.

"And so, the stroll of the ex-morgue assistant and the highly experienced woman has come to its logical conclusion..." stated Nikolai confusedly.

"Do you mean we have arrived at the station, or you won't see me anymore because I am so experienced?"

"No, neither…"

"It's getting chilly…"

"I'd give you something to throw on your shoulders, but…"

"I'd refuse… You don't understand me very well. I'm not a loose woman, and I wasn't planning on dragging you into bed…"

"Oh, that would be very tempting…"

"Really? But, I am married…"

"Husbands can be replaced…"

"No, I'm not like that. I just wanted to look you over…"

"To test me?"

"Well, not exactly… I just wanted to know what sort of person you were."

"So, now do you know?"

"No… I think you have many layers."

"I don't think so."

"Well, there's my tram."

"I'm going with you, I'll get off in three stops for my bus. It will be easy for me to get home that way!

"Let's go…"

They entered into a half-empty car.

"So, where were we?"

"On how I turn you on…"

"How did you work that out?"

"Because you were definitely going the other direction, but you got on this tram so that you could spend a couple more minutes with me…" she clearly liked to bait him.

"Absolutely not. It's faster on the bus."

"So you mean that I don't turn you on?"

"Again checking my integrity?"

"How am I testing your loyalty? Then again, I'd like to take a shower…"

"Together?"

"Well, I love it when my back is rubbed, only I don't like it when I get molested," confided Mira with a laugh.

"I swear that in the tub I would conduct myself decently, and only pay attention to your back…"

"So, as far as you think, I am so dirty that I need a good scrubbing?"

"You're not dirty."

"What am I?"

"Cute"

"A very interesting answer… Isn't it about time for you to get off? See you… Don't take it all so seriously… I was joking. I just didn't want a sappy old-fashioned walk …"

"Turned out to be state-of-the art… So it was all a joke? You're not married?"

"What does it matter?"

Stepping off the streetcar, he turned around trying to get a glimpse of Mira. He noticed an insubstantial movement and decided that she was waving her hand goodbye. The tram had thundered off for some time, but he still stood perplexedly in the breezy square.

"Let's see now… Did she really like me or was she messing with me? "Definitely, for sure it was all lies… She had fifteen lovers… And she's married… She could just be a slut. Any my ears just about fell off. My god she's cute… so cute… But look, she's out of my league... If the hat doesn't fit, or how does that expression go?..."

It absent-mindedly crossed the square and meandered over to the stop in order to in the other direction. He really did not go in the right direction to be with her. In the streetcar, after sitting down in an available seat, Nikolai surrendered himself to the normal flow of thoughts, which were very different from the ideas that flew out of his month and into his surroundings. He knew that if he let himself go that they would put him back into the psychiatric ward again, as they did when he evaded the army draft. There it was not necessary to put on a pretense: he just simply had to consent to his own usual private show while keeping control of his tongue. In the military the outcome of this questionable experiment was put down to schizophrenic delirium. Talented people frequently are written off as mentally deranged. So much simpler. Surer. At least, for the others. However, Nikolai was hardly crazy in the full sense of the word. Simply the train of his thoughts continuously consisted of unexpected sentences, and not amazingly, because he was not so much an inherent philosopher, but rather an intense poet, and his inner thoughts were much sharper than his ordinary, usual talk.

"Mira, Mira… Is it possible that have stupidly fallen in love? All at once, inevitably? Why this simple hysteria? Absurd! Its possible that I like this girl, that's all, but I don't intend to be distracted at all… Infatuation inevitably leads to distraction. Life never tires of testing me with surprises." For the rest of the morning all was simple and mundane, he was laid-back, and the night's rest, that ancient master of healing, completely refreshed him. He had an intense dream, with a somewhat fantastic scenario, wherein Minerva seemed to have landed in his bed. And without much of a fight, gave herself to him… Hey… Its not Minerva, but a cross between a news anchor lady and.. "Oh my God! It's the one I dreamed I met yesterday, Mira! Or is this what it seems?" Yet, one way or another, the next morning he was ready to face the world in calm contemplation. True his living sword was ready this morning, hungrily wishing to plunge into something real, rather than an imaginary sheath, but the indolent logic of compulsory abstention forced him to calm the living crossbow that always distracts him from the hustle and bustle of daily life. He simply wrapped his palm around it and went back to sleep again, and when he awoke, the flood of unrealizable dreams had subsided, everything was cool; and he got out of bed contemplating the aspects of health in his life. Having risen, eaten and partaken of his morning ablutions… "Thank God for my animal existence… every morning the hard world dictates to me, its hard rules, and I am almost happy and satisfied with myself… But now everything has fallen into disarray… I need that girl, as if I was born only for her, to look into those wildly laughing eyes! Nonsense… She's not for me… What stupidity. And yet how is this possible? What in the hell have my hormones done, these flights of erotic fantasy in the bed sheets instead of in the clouds?... My brain, like a slightly stimulated clitoris, can no longer think of anything except candlelit dinners, quite whispers, stolen love… My juices lead me to the bitter pill that I am on the scent of this bitch. Where are they, those denizens of disreputable parlors? Where are the shining Casanovas, Don Juans?... The ancient Chinese recommended that one spend the night with a minimum of ten women, and to give not one of them one's seed… I would give all to just one. I don't need seven! Or, how many according to the Chinese saying? It means nothing to me. Hey, where are you, my gurus?... Teach me about this feather… Exactly- Mira is a feather, so light, so ethereal… And its not that she's so beautiful… but despite those plain looks, my African cork is filled with flames of the Aurora borealis, escape from which could be just a really good blow job, can be the true heaven of youth, where the search for a moist and tooth-filed search can bring one to singular pleasure. Lust, this credo of an erection brings a new era. Only us Russian woodpeckers, living in this god-forsaken part of the world at the end of the 20th century, consider each other as sexless comrades, companions in this land… In the meantime, the phallus, the Lingam… call it what you want… it, it is the king of all cults. And it fears neither artificial monsters nor dangerous possibilities, nor catching and letting daylight on to the jumbled hunt for the doe…"

The tram rattled, and Nikolai again returned his internal attention to its restless counterpart.

"There it is, my blunted Lingam… My unique, brainless, and audacious friend, and the cause of my misfortunes! It is a simple happiness that my thoughts are not heard by any mocking editors… It would be a lustful presentation like the first horrors of an overripe virgin. Books – they are the mass grave of hidden ideas…"

On the next day, he did not see her until noon, although he could not get her out of his head for one minute. No sooner than he was in the lunch line when he met his challenger from yesterday, and started to feel a slight annoyance, which – and he was splendidly aware of this – could not be otherwise like the feeling of the fox, the very some mangy fox from the fable, "And where did she get this idea that she turns me on? Her ass is flat… Breasts are too small. And from what can see, not so smart. An overconfident bubblehead…" But when it came that Mira said smiling: "Ah, its lucky that you turned up… It won't be so dull waiting for the meal", how quickly his irritation melted away, and Nikolai felt he could not resist her charm.

The line was a half-hour long, not less, and so it was necessary to start up a conversation. Mira glanced at him almost tenderly and stayed silent.

"How is the family?" he asked as if with concern, still hoping that the marriage of Mira was nothing more than a figment of imagination.

"Fine, thanks… As always…" answered Mira, and then she said something that caused Nikolai to loss all hope.

"My husband molested me… There was nothing to do but give in. To me he is neither flesh nor fowl, but he insisted… For all that, generally he is boring… No, not exactly. A very boring person. I usually sleep completely without clothes, so that my skin can breathe better; but last night I especially went directly to bed dressed, so as to avoid being molested. But he insisted…"

Nikolai felt that Mira wasn't joking, although he did not understand how he had earned such, one would think, an indiscreet or, what's worse, an intentional disclosure: it was as if she were allowing him to grab this thread and use it to pull the relationship onto a different, closer, more intimate level. He tried to come off with a joke.

"We have not had time to get to know each other, and already you've failed me…And on top of that with whom… with your own husband! How seedy!"

He looked directly into the eyes of Mira, but nothing out of the normal was in her regard. Just a normal look as if the conversation dealt with trading notes or even any other trivial university issue.

"Well, of all things, no one's called me seedy before."

"But have you told everyone that you sleep naked?"

And again, her answer perplexed him.

"No, only you," she said, and then asked unexpectedly: "Why did you decide to study philosophy?"

"I had to study something…" Nikolai mumbled indistinctly.

"Is that it?"

"Really? I hate philosophy…" he confessed all at once.

"Really… that's a good reason…"

"I mean modern philosophy. Seneca once said, that the study of philosophy means finding the path to human happiness, or something like that. But what has modern philosophy turned into – a joke about man and his undiscovered fortune. And what is debated by today's philosophers? Popular issues about which its unlikely that they even understand completely themselves. And what do we get from the answers to these questions? And is it even possible that they can find reasonable compromises between the opposing sides? And will it make anyone happy?"

"And did you your Seneca make anyone happy?"

"At least he asked the question… Or else, for example, there's Epicurus… And you know," he suddenly asserted, "maybe he nevertheless made people happy…"

"Well, anyways, he didn't make you happy…"

"Why?" he choked.

"You don't look like a happy person…"

"Why?" he said again.

"How could a person really be happy without solid and genuine love?" Mira intensely looked him in the eye, and he quickly looked away.

"Who are you? George Sand, who was ready to seduce miserable Chopin's body, and therefore by the same token… well its not important, but in the end killed off his musical soul?"

"I told you, I am tired of Chopin… And why are you always implying that I am trying to seduce you?... Oh now, what a prude!" Mira naughtily pursed her lips."

"Oh, I am entirely for it, if you were to seduce me..." Nikolai quickly corrected enthusiastically. "I have never -

... been popular wit persons of the opposite sex. I even wrote the following: 'I will never wear fancy hats, and never love beautiful women'..."

"Don't flatter yourself... The fact that I like you doesn't completely mean that you will go over big with others... I don't have bad taste, but rather a perverse preference, this is a well-known fact, lest you denigrate other girls."

"Girls don't love me!" Nikolai tried to comically intone through his nose, but it came out sounding phony and unfunny.

"What's the good of other women? I love you," Mira said quietly as if to herself.

What is this? Did he hear right, was she saying that she loved him? So quickly, just like that? In the lunch line? It shouldn't happen that way. At least to him, it happened that way once already. His first love started her affair with him like this – they met on the stairs when she suddenly and directly said: "I love you"... In truth that love-affair did not go much further. Other relationships ended with the refrain: " Sorry, Nikolai, it would seem I made a mistake..." And then, after repeated failures of his amorous intentions, gradually his youthful love gave way to inebriation with his friend Mikhail. Nikolai would forgive them, set up meetings with them, but they would not show up; and so he would place the roses he had bought for her onto one of many graves in the cemetery next to the park.

"So you've taken philosophy in order to kill it, to destroy it, so to speak, from within?"

Mira, it seemed, was surprised at herself that she had blurted out the words "I love you…", which however she did not want to turn into a joke.

"But you do believe that any act must be for a specific purpose? I, in general, do not have a very enthusiastic opinion about myself, and rather, I simply react to life, instead of fulfilling huge goals…" he explained toneless and entirely without formality.

"That's good, that you are modest… I don't like vanity…" Mira concluded.

"Ok, so lets follow that question with a question… Why did you end up in philosophy in our local mill?"

"Do you want the real story or the official version?" inquired Mira before answering.

"Let's start with the official one…" muttered Nikolai, who was already shaken by the open frankness of the girl.

"OK… According to the official version, I plan to better the world…"

"And the unofficial version?"

"Woman-philosopher – this is nonsense… In such a way, I am trying to sweeten my feminine assets.. as usual… My dream is to find happiness or at least to rescue myself from the dreary world of apartments, diapers, and dishes…"

"Honest and tasteful!"

"Does my openness shock you?" Mira innocently looked down.

" Oh, absolutely not… Actually the opposite…" Nikolai answered somewhat off the mark, and this did not escape the notice of his observant partner.

"How is it the opposite? If it does not shock you, then what?"

"Well, if you stated to the acceptance committee that the main reason of your visit within these walls is to escape from your impotent husband…"

"He is absolutely not impotent. Sometimes he even hurts me because he's not impotent. Really, he can't do it more than once, but from that one time its enough to put a pistol to one's head from all the thrusting…"

"And you don't like that?"

"Ugh, Nikolai, you are still a little boy… Women aren't only interested in that…"

"Well, since I won't turn into a woman any time soon, why don't you tell me, the little boy, what woman want?" asked Nikolai stubbornly.

"It's a well-known fact… Romance… Love… Tenderness… It's only in porno films where ravishment is all that matters… We women are built differently…"

"Really? Then how did we both end up in the philosophy department?" Smiled Nikolai. "Indeed it seems that Hegel suggested that the difference between men and women as the same as that between plants and animals."

"I agree with Hegel."

"Oho!"

"Yes, if you please, I agree… Women are more sensual and therefore completely dependent on their emotions… They cannot come to reasonable decisions in big politics, science…"

"But men can? I can't believe my ears," Nikolai began to laugh. "Such ideas I would expect to hear from the mouths of misogynists, a brute, a construction worker… Maybe, you're just kidding?"

"Well, in every joke there is a bit of truth…" Mira playfully teased her hair. "Why are all the great philosophers man? Do you actually believe that women, those tremulous, shrill creatures, could produce a good philosopher, or, to be more precise, a 'philosophress'?

"You should read a little Hume, on his theme on modesty… There it is explained in laymen's terms, why a woman should only have one partner, while a man should have as many as he chooses…"

"I don't remember anything like that from Hume... although to be honest it seems I did not read Hume... only excerpts."

"Oh, excerpts can be misleading..."

"But do you think that also, that a woman should only have one partner?"

"Well, I am an interested party..."

"In what are you interested?"

"Well, you did understand mean when I said you turn me on..."

"Which is to say that you propose that I, judging by sight of it – a perfectly modest girl, ... Well, OK, OK... a perfectly modest girl become your lover?"

"Why not... Hegel and Hume, as with all human beings, suffer from prejudices, attacks of ignorance and complacency... while I, please observe, consider women not only equal to men, but also more beautiful, interesting, and multi-faceted..."

"This is because you have thus far not had one... I fear you change your opinion...."

"Possibly... Definitely, it is necessary to think about all this. Thinking is a generally highly useful pastime... And then its possible to think about something that never came to the mids of Hume and Hegel."

"So you don't believe in the classics?"

"Not at all…" Nikolai stood in the pose of a Roman orator and added: "I am my own authority!"

"Well. It was Descartes who stated that we should check all with our own intellects…"

"Oh, I am a true follower of Descartes…" he suddenly became silent, and then he sharply squeezed out from his suddenly dried-up throat: "How I would love you on a pile of books…"

"What, what? This is something new… Or did I hear it right?" Mira's voice disintegrated into an entire avalanche of barely control giggles. "Here you are… beginnings on Hume, and ended on…"

"I'm not finished yet…"

"Don't become attached to the words. Sick puppy," Mira waved her hand and accidentally slapped Nikolai in his privates; and instantly he felt a simple, unbearable rush, like a ray of sunshine, emanating from that point and even more carnal desire. He barely knew how to hide the obvious external signs of his feelings, and took a step back and tried to take his attention away from the sudden swelling.

"Please believe me, mademoiselle, nothing so stimulates me as a conversation on philosophy with a pretty lady!"

"I see…" whispered Mira and gracefully averted her gaze. She clearly did not expect such a living reaction to her prank.

"So, why are all the philosophers men?" Nikolai was a bit foggy, but he tried to hide it. "I think these are throwbacks to the past. Now you yourself are a living example of, well, feminism, that is. Instead of hanging out at home with the dishes."

"Well, whoever hangs out, still needs to look out…" Mira unexpectedly began to laugh and glanced back at his crotch. Everything had settled down, and she feigned a disappointed sniff: "Love has gone, the tomatoes have withered…"

Nikolai had had enough and decided to close in.

"You were deliberately trying to get me turned on!"

Mira pursed her lips and responded.

"How did you get that?... It was totally not that at all. Unless you are inclined to study Tantric sex…"

"What kind of sex?"

"Tantric! It is when he is on one side of the city, and she is on the other. He watches TV, and she does the laundry… But it is impossible to cum… It is very erotic. Want to try?.."

Finally, having finished the meal, the young philosophers left the cafeteria. The meal caused in them considerably less emotion than the preceding conversation.

β

In the evening Nikolai went over to see Mikhail. His friend was fun to hang out with and a non-stop wind-bag; but, perhaps, it was only with him with whom it was possible to have a serious discussion; and true, he himself had no lack of outrageous deficiencies. Mikhail was a free artist, and had dropped out of school in the ninth grade, while for several years had already been making money by reconstructions; he painted icons in the old style… He was a genius. Of his erudition Mikhail excelled over all others, and his creative potential was such that from when it first showed itself… everyone would whisper: "Something is still to come!"

Nikolai did not hurry to lay out the tale of his sudden love to Mikhail. In this there was a selfish interest. It was necessary to at the minimum hang out, for forms sake… to while away at the pad, so to say… And the apartment of Mikhail was a most agreeable place. Nikolai knew that there that was a bottle of vodka that would surely be offered in this linen covered apartment… Mikhail for the most part time lived alone, since his mother, who was divorced, very often absented herself on "business trips", and they had long ago divided the living space into two separate warring camps, shutting away the other half with lock and key. They even had separate refrigerators!

Nikolai began in a roundabout way, but instead of listening and sympathizing Mikhail, after smoking some hand-rolled cigarettes, got onto his hobby horse. He considered himself to be an earnest Socrates and loved to philosophize with the philosophers, assuming that he very elegantly knocks downs these demagogues using their own arguments. After listening to the story about the feelings of Nikolai, he thoughtfully questioned:

"How is it possible to distinguish, that the fact that we in actuality do feel, from the fact that to us it only seems as if we feel?"

"What do you mean by that?" Nikolai specified vacantly, already feeling sorry that he had shared his thoughts with Mikhail. You couldn't beat anything smart out of this wind-bag. And so the babble continued.

"Well, for example, you think that you have fallen in love, while actually you just want to sleep with her, and you think from that it is falling in love, but in reality it isn't… I know, I know… Now you will demand the reasons from me… What I do understand of the concept 'to want to fuck' while on the other hand 'to be in love'? In other words, as the proverb says, 'without the bottle… the head is dust!', or, to be more precise, 'without the bottle… life is no fun!'"

"Don't joke around… How about a drink – as they say… But no – don't burden my soul…"

"There's always a drink," Mikhail said victoriously, after reaching into the shelf for an unopened bottle wheat vodka. "Now I have to grab a sausage. I have a Doktorskaya sausage in my refrigerator. Doctors absolutely recommend to have it with the vodka… Studies show that this leads to the growth and formation of grains of wheat in the stomach, allowing the vodka to go to the head faster, bread after all, brother, everything to the head!

"Whoa, Mikhail, Mikhail, if you could only hear from the other side, what bullshit you are…"

"And how long has it been now since you've been released from the nut house?" Mikhail gently snapped, who had also been cut from the army, from asserting that he regularly consorted with real angels.

"And from where do you always get a bottle?"

"There are some good people…"

"You, Mikhail, not only do you dabble in icons, but you even take vodka for it! Christ-seller, in other words!"

"Hey. Don't mess with my Jewish roots… I'm Hebrew only through my mother!" Mikhail muttered and poured out vodka into two teacups, since not another clean dish was to be found in the kitchen.

After a dink the friends snacked on the sausage. Nikolai peevishly said:

"So, here you were asking how is it possible to distinguish, that the fact that we in actuality do feel, from the fact that to us it only seems as if we feel? It seems me, as in the majority of cases, that you're asking the wrong question… So therefore it is not possible to be satisfactorily answered."

"That's how you answer most of my questions…"

"Unfortunately, most of the time the problem is exactly in the way you ask the question. If the wrong question is asked, then one should not try to answer it."

"And so what should I do?"

"Either ask another question, or just drop this them altogether, if you cannot ask an intelligent question."

"That's all fine and good, but can you tell me what was wrong with my question? Can you at least tell me that? Mikhail was starting to get irritated.

"Well, OK. Simply speaking, without the demagoguery so abhorrent to you, so feelings - first, if something seems to us or we think of something, then, at least from our point of view, then no other point of view in reference to the fact that we feel is legitimate. Since we ourselves are the sole arbiters of ourselves!

"Do not say that. For example, let's examine pain… Let us suppose pain is subjective, but indeed its shown from observation… That yes, even torture, after all, acts on almost everybody to rejuvenate him!"

"That's precisely it, pain!" took up Nikolai. "The sensation of pain is much more easily analyzed than the being of love… Although there exists something universal between these two troubles, of course…" he opined, entering into the flow of the conversation. He again felt himself at his peak. Now, when his reality consisted of a bottle and the smoke of a cigarette, Mira seemed to be a distant morning vision. "If we without poetry, then pain, however it may be subjective, is nevertheless manifested in everyone by more or less similar means, not like love… Sometimes we perceive pain or, for example, happiness, but we do not completely realize it. That is to say, the feeling remains at the subconscious level. Therefore there are two levels of perception: deep, and unknown, where it is not possible for the sensation to penetrate, and conscious, where we exactly think that it hurts, and we analyze our feelings."

"But sometimes it happens that pain appears by itself when there are no reasons for its appearance… Like, for example, the phantom pain, when an arm is amputated, and patient still complains of pain in his fingers…" objected Mikhail.

"And what if the best part of the soul were amputated?" joked Nikolai.

"We agreed to do without the poetry…" Mikhail as Nikolai, wrote reasonably good verse, but he considered this occupation worthless.

"Then here precisely it turns out that pain exists, if we are conscious of it, regardless of the fact whether there is a reason for it or not. For this very reason, if we feel that we have fallen in love, then this means, we have fallen in love, although it is also possible to have fallen in love without realizing it…" said Nikolai as he felt that was beginning to contradict himself.

"There you go, you are mixed up!" rejoiced Mikhail. "It means, it is possible to have fallen in love without realizing it, while at the same time it is obvious to those around you. Well, well, so then why was my question not valid?"

"Yes the whole point is that the question was to be able to distinguish that the fact that we in actuality feel, from the fact that it seems to us, as if we feel, is pointless, since, after summarizing it in light of the facts that we have discussed, it turns out that: how it is possible to distinguish from the fact that we do feel, from what we feel? Do you get the nonsense?"

"Honestly speaking, no!"

"The thing is that you assume that there is a certain real facet of a feeling onto which appear internal sensations. But in actuality this is not so…"

"Why?"

"Because those who do not rise to the level of consciousness, i.e., a sensation, about which we know nothing, is not a sensation. Look, gastric juices are produced inside you, but if you are healthy and do not suffer from heartburn, you don't feel anything about it. The sensation, which is not perceived is not a sensation at all. Do you understand?"

"The object of love can cause a repressed thrill of excitement, just barely conscious, and it can express itself into a Shakespearean sonnet, which has written about this feeling for centuries… Although it is necessary to note that aside from two or three sonnets, its about time to throw William's legacy into the trash… Where was I? Ah, yes! The manifestation of a feeling can be very different…”

“But in either case it is not possible to differentiate from that the fact that we feel, and that we only think that we feel… Although let’s see, it seems me that I am beginning to understand the essence of your question…”

“Finally!”

“You have in mind a false interpretation of the sensations: this is what happens when we want to fuck, and our consciousness forces us to believe, where we want to create images, a sort of infamous sublimation, masquerading as an impulse… But in my case it seems everything is clear… It doesn’t matter what I want, if only she exists, she breathes, she lives… Poetry? Love? I don’t give a damn… But those are my feelings.”

The vodka was nearing its end. Mikhail became increasingly more prone to yawning expressively, and Nikolai, after taking his leave with an unstable gait, was thrown out of the apartment into the white light…

He was late to the first lecture and, boldly after piling into the audience, decisively proceeded to the place where she sat. Mira smiled and wanted to say something, but, after being told down by the instructor humbly became silent.

Nikolai sank down into the chair next to her. It did not escape his devoted attention that the girl changed. Which is to say that basically she seemed to be the same playful girl of yesterday, but heaven or hell… in short, who can explain it… well, let us say, the devil, as the saying goes, lies in the details. Many women are capable of changing themselves to the point that their skill borders on the reincarnation of great artists, and not just in certain features, but even in different proportions. Nikolai did not immediately understand the secret of what comprised the change that had come about, and only by breaking down the details, he realized that Mira had exerted special efforts in order to appear so - ordinary for everybody, but it was completely irresistible for him.

She used make-up so skillfully, and also with such taste, that its presence was practically unnoticeable. Only a noticeable blush shaded the pretty oval of her face, making it even more attractive. The tender slope of forehead transitioned into the profile of her slight snub nose, bill, sweet lips led to her chin, which sharply withdrew to her neck. Shadows on her eyelids were moderately dark, the eyebrows were accurately trimmed, and the eyelashes were tinted… Only now he noted that Mira's eyes were hazel. Nikolai's eyes were almost the same color, and he, honestly speaking, did not like the color of his eyes, considering it as being too dramatic, but in designing the face of Mira God gave this color a special beauty and intelligence. The pink nuances of the slightly gleaming lipstick made her lips prominent and expressive.

Nikolai did not love vulgarly made-up women, and the delicate craftsmanship Mira had applied to the natural beauty of her face gladdened him so, as if it had conveyed some exceptionally pleasant news to him.

Her hair style also attested to the fact that a professional stylist worked on it, one who knew something of the fine skill of seduction. The color of Mira's hair tended slightly to reddish, and only that if light hit it at a specific angle, and this ambiguity of color caused an exciting feeling of ambiguity. The curve of her neck stripped him from his mind. It was thin and looked as if it would focus special attention to the velvetiness of her skin. The thin gold chain, on which negligently hung a little heart, made in halves, led from there, downward, to the intoxicating cut of the blouse, which was white at first glance, but on active contemplation revealed tender gray strip on it. The cut descended to the first of two fastenings, and from there, to Nikolai, who viewed it from the side, there was visible the very edge of the side of her breast and even one of the secret birth marks, the existence of which the usual mortal must not know… It could not be said that the bust was provocatively deep. Simply from that point, which Nikolai observed to himself, that to him were now open certain hidden angles, which began to inflame him even more than the breast itself covered by the bulging garments.

To it everything seemed inconceivable. Is there really hidden under this garment a naked body, tender and desired? He could not imagine it to himself, although his entire burdened philosophical mind strained. What is there, under this accursed, yet sweet garment? What form does her breast take without the undergarments? Large nipples or small? Pinkish and round or like the color of skin and flat? These riddles occupied he more than questions of the existence of god and freedom of choice, about which the lecturer boringly and monotonically harped on. Yes and how could he could think about other things, when in all just a few centimeters from the tips of his fingers - the zippers, which lead straight to the very thing of the reality of her true nature. And what about her belly button? – Nikolai could not calm down. He absolutely could not imagine his beloved being naked, to him it even seemed that she was born in that blouse, jeans and black between-season shoes… But well somewhere must be her naked heels, and knees? But it cannot be so, without all this she would not exist?

The gaze of Nikolai fell to her hands and perplexedly it stopped at her engagement ring. The husband - here is a happy fellow, to whom lead the answers to the riddle of all these insoluble questions. How does the depression in the land appear where the spine ends and begins to turn into the ass?

Mira perceived, while he did not make contact with her eyes, and intentionally made the appearance as if he were attentively listening to the lecture, nevertheless literally bathed herself in the waves of his reverent attention.

When lecture finally ended, they, while having uttered not a word, went down into the coatroom, hurriedly put on their coats, left, crossed the square area and sat down on a bench. Mira pulled him by the hand.

"Kiss me, please…" she quietly asked and closed her eyes.

The heart of Nikolai was beating like a capture finch. He was barely breathing as his lips touched her lips. Mira sighed quietly. He moved away carefully.

"Again!" she whispered.

The cracked asphalt of pavements measured the way under the feet of Nikolai and Mira. They forgot all about the their cares and wandered, without any fixed direction. And so it happens, when the grayness of life unexpectedly collides with a new reality. People fall into a zombie state and wander off somewhere by themselves…

"We need to find some kind of shelter…" Mira said, squeezing up against Nikolai.

"Yes, yes… I thought about that… I will try to arrange something soon…"

"No, I didn't mean that… Although… Never mind.. Hold on," Mira suddenly squeezed his hand to the point of pain, so that he wanted to break free, but he bore it. "I wanted to say that the danger, which is concealed in any shelter, this is the danger we must avoid… I don't want to lie, to sneak, or to hide!"

"We must put ourselves to the test…" he answered seriously, and then added: "Even though its temporary…"

"Any minute now we will begin a glorious comparison of mothers and husbands towards a tendency to poison our happiness," sighed Mira.

"Your absurd marriage - accidental product of the approaching apocalypse, and your husband is the doorkeeper-cannibal."

"Let's not talk about him…"

"All this does not mean anything. Only you have meaning."

"I believe that we will be happy. In spite of everything! Yes, I know that sooner or later we will be happy!"

"You are my home valley… I want to settle in it and never leave it! Your hands are so strange, and yet so dear at the same time. To kiss them is like sipping pure champagne…"

Passing by unromantic puddles, Nikolai joked:

"Hail to spies! After being moistened on the streets and in the alleys, they leave each other secret markers like dogs."

"Yes already… In this world the best of anything is adapted precisely for spies. It seems to me, that all of our lecturers are agents of intelligence agencies…"

"Don't say it… Our lectures - these are the attack of imbeciles, the instructors – leaking from the brains flukes. To me I don't need neither philosophy, nor glory nor enlightenment. Everything that I want… No, "I want" - this is too self-reliant… Everything, on which I rely, is here in the touch of our hands," Nikolai quietly said as he tenderly stroked the tips of his finger on Mira's palm.

"Here we have become the latest is a series of convicts of love. As if we were in possession of infection by an unknown bacilli, we wander around the city, threatening to infect incorruptible Petersburg by this reckless magic…" Mira smiled sadly, and it seemed that out of the tail of her eyes it became shiny with tears.

"Yes, we live here and it seems to us, that this is a simple city… No. This city cannot be surprised by anything… It saw much, about which even the most terrible historical books hush up… Building in the swamps… Corpses… Blockade… again corpses everywhere… Yes all in all anything is possible… Our city eternally rules over the bandit peacemakers. My clandestine mentality will one of these days be able to digest its history."

"And entirely amongst this deathly granite - our tiny bubble of happiness! It is impossible!" Mira stopped and began to gaze at the Neva river.

"Yes… the Hermitage delivers entertaining baths, and critic-woodlice as before fuck geniuses in all the openings of their bare skulls, or else everyone indulges himself in the cocaine jail of ecstasy…"

"You are speaking so strangely…" Mira said wonderingly.

"Do I frighten you?"

"No, no, I want to listen to you. The sounds of your voice… They – are wonderful. Speak, speak… Its as if you give birth to verses… You – are my Mandelstam… You are my unique and inimitable genius."

"This is an illusion…" Nikolai began to laugh dramatically, although to him it was pleasant.

"No – this is the only reality accessible!" Mira snuggled against him and quietly sighed: "Why does this city need the current therapeutic plague, blazing in the fires of striptease hell, matrons, who poisoned macaronis… Why don't adults play with toys? Like dolls, for example?"

"Because they have other entertainments… For example, a vagina gifted with artistic skill…" she broke away from Nikolai, and he grew cold. Would this suddenly offend Mira? For the first time he had become so close with the girl, and it was difficult to control himself with her.

"Yuck… how unappealing, but at the same time how true…" Mira agreed unexpectedly. "You know, with my husband I almost always making a pretense in bed, but with you I don't need to make love… I am always on the peak of bliss!"

"I do not believe in married bliss… At least, in this city of ideological opressors and idiotic countrymen In any family the husband invariably becomes the tormenting vampire. Love withers in the gray clutches of the Sunday disease known as 'Take away the garbage!'"

"I believe in married bliss… with you!"

"Petrarch asserted that the ones in love do not have any and should not be under one roof…" said Nikolai and he thought: "How strange, that she said that, as if she were free and ready to leave and marry me…"

As if she read his thoughts and after being freed from his embraces, Mira started to swing her hands and to recite:

Passionate parrot

Recited poetry of Petrarch,

Which he heard

On the radio one day.

Passionate parrot

Dreamed about a blue jay,

Which he saw

Out the window one day.

Passionate parrot

Thought he was in love,

Though he thought for long

What does this word portend?

Recited poetry of Petrarch,

Which he did not apprehend,

Dreamed about a blue jay,

Who he did not know...

"How remarkable! These are your verses?"

"No, some girl composed them…"

"Nevertheless it was wonderful!"

"Yes, we had the luck to be born here, where everything breathes in verse!"

"Contradictory city. I got tired of it… The city, where Pushkin's ghost wanders along the streets and here, next, uprising freaks spews out of its squadron throats the slogans: 'Stop the swamp!' while they themselves eternally pull us into the brutal swamp…"

"Read me one of your verses…"

Nikolai thought.

"Well. Here's one about Petersburg…"

The city died.

Quiet reigned.

Book in taters, and voices dulled

Quartered quatrains,

Abortive abbreviations.

The brain is battered. It seems pointless,

Immured into a glazed tile.

The palace square convulses

Triumphant nonsense. Speak!

Justify! Wasn't it us who prayed,

Till we grew mute, and bit our lips blue

In Blood, "…in nominee patri, et filii

Et spiritus sancti.." – Amen!

Right only the one who comes to judge. Perhaps darkly

Are there behind the bars five fingers?

But the effect from the separated bridges

Generates a bad appetite.

By hand the shroud is torn to pieces,

And desecrated in the white night

The City of Peter, the city of ditches –

The tomb is deserved. It died. Silence.

"It is good, but it is horrible…"

"Then I will write entirely different verses…"

"Different?"

"Yes, about you… From now on all my verses will be only about you…"

"How nice!" Mira happily smiled and trustingly snuggled against his arm.

δ

In the meanwhile the city plunged into twilight; and it became necessary for them to part. After leaving Mira, Nikolai went straight to Mikhail's place and asked him directly, without any fuss, to lend him the key for just a couple of hours.

"Well, you are strong, brother," Mikhail husked jealously. He smoked a lot – exclusively the "Belomor" brand. Mikhail himself usually never slept with the same woman more than once since he considered this to be a bad taste and a huge waste of time…. In spite of his young years, he could compete with the best lady's men and claim the doubtful laurels of being the best at it in that category. He looked older than his age, with his thick beard "a la Karl Marx" and simply drove women to hysterics.

"Will you introduce me to her?" he slyly asked, already knowing the answer.

"No… You would seduce her, and then I'd have to kill you…"

"That again…" sighed Mikhail, as he smoked a cigarette.

"What do you mean, 'that again'?"

"You'd have to kill me again!" winked Mikhail.

Apart from the first love of Nikolai, Mikhail had stolen several potential girlfriends away from him a few times. This did not keep them from staying friends throughout the years.

A get-together would be arranged, two girls invited, and it would all end up with Nikolai going home alone, and Mikhail sleeping with both of them. The shyness of Nikolai, his ordinary appearance, and his confused and difficult way of talking interfered with simple everyday relationships…

"But, please hide your shabby pants, since the poor contents of your closet are always scattered all over the place," whined Nikolai, out of sorts because of Mikhail's wink.

"That's OK, that's fine… your "nymph" won't even notice the chaos… Loving one woman is like a funeral…"

"What do you mean?"

"Well. Is there any difference where your unborn life will end up, either in a real graveyard or a condom?.. And in both cases, life has ended, and is it really important at what stage! Is there any difference who will bury your unborn offspring? By the way, if you feel the need to use a rubber, it is in the desk drawer…"

"Do you mean an eraser?"

"Well if you can stretch it and put it on, then you're right…"

"So, are you keeping your condoms in a desk drawer? What an original place to keep them…"

"Well, I am sorry… Where am I supposed to keep them? In the bank? I don't have a nightstand, as you can see… Poverty…"

"I wish I were as poor as you…"

"Also, there is some deodorant in the desk drawer, if you are burning all the bridges of your innocence…"

"Why?"

"Because virgins don't use deodorants for their underarms."

"Nonsense!" Nikolai said angrily.

"And that's what I say, it's total nonsense…" agreed the artist.

"You know, everything you say is a strange reflection of our true thoughts… And in those words there is an endless struggle with imbecilic doubts…" mumbled Nikolai.

"So what's your problem? Are you afraid that you will fail? Well, it happens when it's the first time…But she, as I understand, is experienced. And you, most importantly, shouldn't think too much about it…"

"You have very simplistic ideas about sex… Love is when the heavenly trumpets…"

"Love is a Chinese massage with a French kiss…" interrupt Mikhail. "I warned you; if you think too much you will disgrace yourself."

"And you are going further and further towards the black hole of depravity…"

Mikhail laughed.

"I have strong feelings! And you, you are a follower of Marquis de Sade, your ideal is bloody fangs, your partners are soldiers of hell, admirers of hairy asses, gay vampires!"

"Are you finished? OK then, you won't get the flat. And make sure to remember: once does not make you gay, and besides, I was dead drunk at the time. I regret that I shared it with you…"

"Shit happens."

"But you are just a bed-wetting dilettante… For you great sex is so distant, as far away as my old ancestors…"

"You are spending too much time with your clients… I mean with your fathers. Or your faggots? So which is it? Your life,

Mikhail, is a bunch of tasteless feasts, recyclable bodies, and hateful houses…"

"Put aside your European neuroses. We are the descendants of wild Huns, who are used to throwing their naked bodies onto ice!"

"You, Mikhail, are the king of chaos! And your friend Paul is a drug dealer!"

"And now I feel like I am going to lapse into the kicking sickness…"

"What sickness?"

"When one needs to kick somebody's ass!"

"You are just jealous of my strong and pure love… Your hairy headpiece is not capable of understanding this concept…"

"Why don't you just piss off?"

"So in short, we are coming over at 10 in the morning…Can you go out for a walk?"

"We, brethren-prostitutes, are used to it. God be with you. Despite the obvious mutations in your logic, even you need some female attention. And here is an anatomical chart. You better study it, to learn…"

"Don't brag so much about your experience! Look at your pad! It reminds me not of a lover's nest, but the lair of an orangutan!"

"You don't know anything of the art of design... Within these surroundings I am inspired with volcanic ideas!"

"And don't they die in your snares, and not trip over your scattered intimate implements?"

"These are all female complaints, but we should unite over our strong male bonds. Remember in sex, a detailed plan is useless; switch off your mind. Otherwise your sausage will be hanging like a deflated balloon!"

"Why are you so worried about my potency? Have you had such a negative experience?"

"And who has not?"

"I am starting to worry. If such a sexual juggernaut like you had problems, then my obvious strength that's bursting at the seams will start to wear away backwards..."

"Orgasm is a lethal cake, and you should earn it. In the anal annals of life everything is set up so inconveniently that the tube-like sweet things are aimed into luxurious crap-houses rather than into the promised nests... This is just an unavoidable hallucination that you and I have ever-ready volunteer vibrators in our pants. Everything is circumstantial, as the stars may dictate...

"You shouldn't be sleeping with a dozen women in seven days..."

"Don't tell me that! Child!"

"Even the worn-out assed Crusaders, the witnesses of the "Creator", spared their spears and did not waste their strength on random sex. Mikhail, you are a heroin God. Instead of supporting me and guiding me into the feeling of friendship and romance, all that you can offer are a few pieces of cheap advice peppered with freshly baked sarcasm… She, by the way, said that she just needs to hear my voice…"

First of all, its not heroin, but cocaine… I don't like heroin... You should know the difference by now… And you are a masochistic hero, a wild prince, the Napoleonic skin of Josephine… I am just trying to warn you… Look, don't burn out as a hopeless nymph lover… Man's weakness, combined with man's lack of sexual satisfaction, is the main scourge of society. It is that, which is responsible for practically all bloody testimonials in history…" Mikhail dove into philosophizing.

"However, quite on the contrary, I always thought that it is the violent libido, masturbation and the like that are responsible."

"No… A sexually satisfied man does not need anything. The world is driven by impotence! And our city, after putting on the wigs of balconies, observes how man's weakness and lack of sexual satisfaction drive them to routine suicides. The fogs are bad for the health… Dampness is deadly… St. Pete has a bad climate. It is good only for criminals and those living in basement solitude…" said Mikhail capriciously.

Nikolai did not say a word and put the key to Mikhail's apartment in his pocket.

"For God's sake, please leave before we come over. The sight of your snout will badly affect the delicacy of the situation…"

"OK, OK…" yawned Mikhail.

After she came home, Mira submerged into her domestic routine, but her soul and her mind were far away. She had been split in two halves for two months. From a stranger's perspective she looked the same, but inside she felt a wierd mixture of detachment and struggling with herself. Despite the hard-won experience of skepticism and "being reasonable", she had a sudden relapse into a sentimental dreamy girl, that she had tried so hard to get rid of for years. She was floating in the aura of this dreaminess, coming back to herself. Nobody, except herself, needed her to be of a high flying nature, and for years she had been building a shield, convenient and understandable to the people around her. But behind the shield a lively soul was starting to die quietly, threatening to turn Mira into a typical boring hag with a regular set of sensations, problems, grievances, and small worthless pleasures. It is so difficult to save one's deep soul, if it is of no use to anyone. It is so laughable and clumsy that even the people who are close to you tend to turn their heads away or in the best case condescendingly try not to notice, or even to urgently advise you to get rid of all romantic feelings and line up in the orderly rows of loud-spoken champions to the universal acclaim of "hag-dom"!

And when you become skillful in pretending and in exterminating the inner "I", so that you become unable to distinguish yourself from the most cynical, sharp-toothed and fanged specimens. But all of a sudden, fate, as if it were laughing at you, throws at you a person or a happenstance, that will revive your inner "I", and all shields and protective armor will turn to ashes, and you find yourself trying hard to save the appearances of similarity to the others. It would be wrong to say that Mira was thinking about all of this turmoil inside of her. But the feelings were so strong that all her strength was devoted to keeping up the appearances. And nobody around her understood her well enough to notice that underneath the daily forms a huge change was taking place in her soul. And it was the very root of her happiness and unhappiness. Happiness, since she was able to sustain the flow of her daily life, without troubling her parents, her husband, or her little son. Unhappiness, because even with a full set of people dear to her, she remained absolutely lonely. And no one cared who in essence Mira was.

Her only hope to reach understanding and emotional closeness was her son. But he was so small that this hope was lost in the uncertainty of the future without relieving the present need. Her son stood as the sole reason for her quiet logical marriage. She really needed a soul, interested exclusively in her – Mira, even at the most basic animal level. And her husband became a logical continuation of the union between Mira and the baby completing the traditional family unit. Due to her immaturity and her weakness, Mira could not overcome her fear of social expectations and concerns of her parents. The husband, in Mira's thinking, was a victim from the start, a fooled party, whom she needed for pragmatic reasons as a shield covering her from the world. Some kind of check mark, a means to create a soul mate. Her husband never became her soul mate. They were too different. Mira saw through him, pitied him and pardoned his shortcomings. She, on the contrary, remained an unpredictable puzzle for him full of unexplained surprises. Both parties engaged in some sort of game imaging themselves and their partner as something else, without revealing any details of an inner nature. Mira tried to perform the role of a caring and thoughtful wife, and played this role with lightness of a basketball champion throwing an apple core into the trash bin and she was conscious of the fact that this pretense would soon bore her to death. And she could not count on any other prospects to put her efforts into because of the limitations of her partner. Mira's husband was engaged in the house and household chores, seriously applying all his fantasy and strength, but the results attained which would normally seem extraordinary to a hypothetical woman, just produced a constrained smile of approval from Mira, as a mother approving the art creation of a three-year old son, which of course deserves approval and encouragement, but it is impossible to decipher what it actually depicts…

It is not surprising that the decision to enroll in the philosophy department was driven by a desperate intellectual hunger and pain, the pain of unapplied strengths and talents which were gradually being covered by the thick crust of routine and the mold of banality.

However, instead of a glorious school of philosophy surrounded by the columns of Plato with passionate discussions and the search for truth, the bold lecturers were spreading bullshit from the lecterns, and there was not a bit of hope of exercising the mind and the soul in what they were saying, without which all scientific terms turn into pitiful nonsense.

In Nikolai Bangushine with her inner sight as if with an X-ray she saw the same worn-down soul trying to find an exit and a soul mate! She was ready to pay for a single word with him by being unlawful to her husband, her mother land, God, to the devil himself… to whomever, to nourish herself, maybe for the fist time in her life, with the joy of the true, non-animalistic, human being!

ζ

The night passed in restless dreams… Nikolai dreamed about tomorrow, how he would bring Mira into the apartment of Mikhail, how they would kiss at first, and then how nothing would stop them, and then finally how he would tear away her loathsome clothing and would kiss every cell of her body, each tiny birth mark… Then all of a sudden he became frightened that something would go wrong, that something would stand in their way, and that something would happen to him. And he, trying not to make any noise, went to the balcony, where blew the unpleasant and sharp wind from the Gulf, and smoked one cigarette after another, until in he had a head ache so strong that it was necessary to wrap his head with a cold wet towel and to take a pair of pills.

He could hardly wait for the morning, and at six in the morning, he solemnly and slowly headed towards the bathroom. After locking the door, he undressed and quickly looked at himself in the mirror. He suddenly shuddered from the thought that this naked, hairy creature with a stooped back and a slightly sagging stomach would present itself in front of her eyes…

"She will hate me! She will simply throw up!" he almost said out loud to himself.

There was a small noise behind the door.

"Why have you gotten up so early?" asked his mother.

"I had a head ache, I could not sleep…" Nikolai shouted out through the door.

"If you keep on smoking, not only your head will fall off."

The words of his mother caused him to think sadly about what else exactly could still fall off. After looking at his private parts, he remained extremely disappointed. In the lax condition his worm resembled a certain invertebrate creature, run over by a bread truck. Of course in other circumstances Nikolai was quite content with his endowment. Once in the morning he arose with it in its complete glory, and he could not resist the temptation to measure it with a ruler. His 4.7 inches frightened him a little because he had read in some book that it should have been 5.9 inches long, or even better 7.1 inches; but after considering the size of an average girl and after taking into account that the modest size of his instrument was compensated by its thickness and could stand proudly and confidently, he decided that he would not be upset and that his instrument would be just fine, plus – as everyone says – size does not matter, and so on.

Today as if in spite, Nikolai was not in his best shape. He even briefly considered canceling the meeting, calling in sick or simply not saying anything to Mira about the key, and to quietly spend the day at the university and, after kissing for a couple of hours in the alleyways, to blissfully and a little bit tiredly to see Mira home.

“No, I should not miss this chance. In the end… if something happens she will understand… But if I am a wimp, then why would she cheat on the husband? Friendship is, of course, important, but when you are kissing conversations usually cease, and therefore, most likely, there is something greater than friendship between the two of us…" Therefore he had to make a decision. Nikolai switched on the tap, and burning hot water slowly trickled down. He added some cold water, and the stream became ice cold. Nikolai irritatedly added some more hot water, and the water again came at a boil.

"What the hell?! In so many thousands of years of civilization people have still not come with anything better…"

"Damn this country…" For some reason he was convinced that abroad the showers were better, and that there were some buttons that could be pushed to get the ideal water temperature.

Nikolai finished the shower with some difficulty. While toweling down he looked at the mirror again. This time he liked his reflection better. So what? Young, healthy body. If he sucked in his stomach, all proportions looked great. Strong hands. Broad chest. Good height. Legs not crooked. What else could he want? Strangely enough, due to all these thoughts and after having examined himself in the mirror, something trembled in his spineless appendage.

"A masturbator and a narcissist," he diagnosed himself angrily, but then in a more cheerful state of mind, he dressed and proceeded to the university.

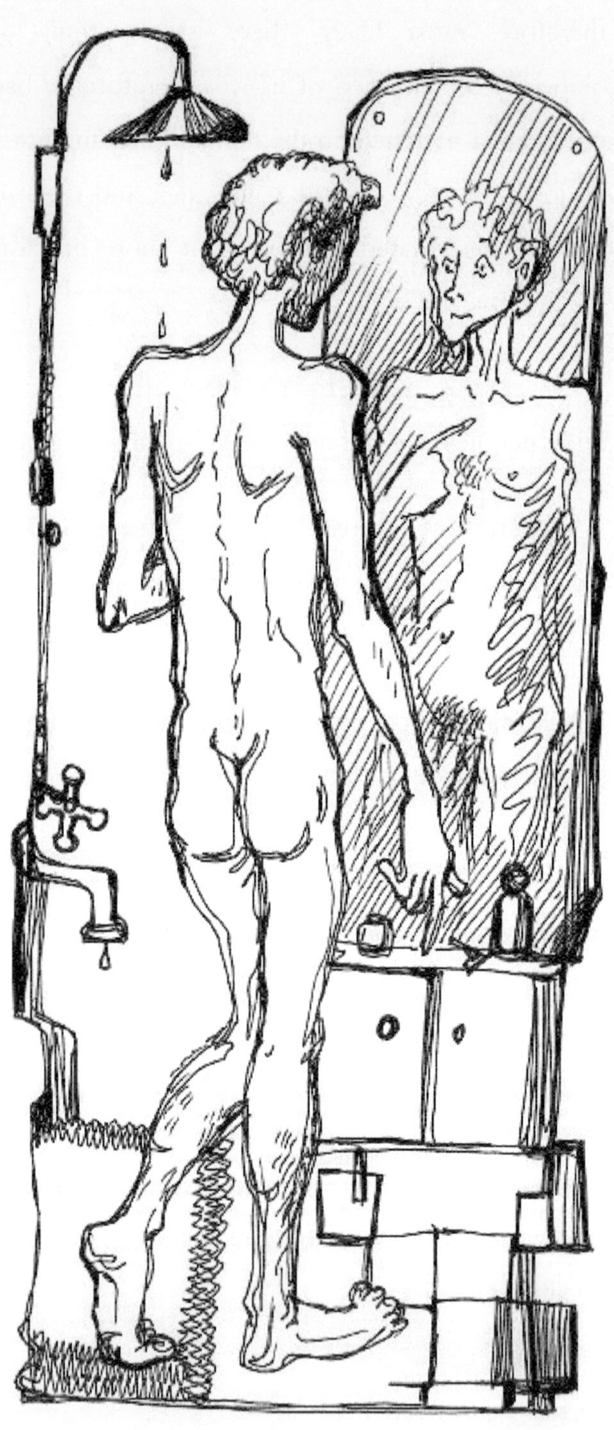

"What if it does not work?" the thought stung him for the last time. "What if Mikhail was not joking? That's stupid… When I kiss – my balls tighten up. How wouldn't it work?... What if she is not that attractive underneath? She had a baby after all. Who knows?"

Nikolai Bangushin was a man with a philosophical bent. He had read Kant and Hegel, and was so wrapped up in these materials that he did not agree with either of them. How did it happen that his thoughts were now more concentrated on his uneasiness about his spineless appendage, his naughty eye dropper, to which nature had given the main role of producing children, more than other role? An interesting thing occurs to people who consider themselves enlightened when they come face to face with the need to live in the materialistic world. The nineties were just beginning, and the people were still not yet corrupted enough or devoted to all the sacraments of the science of lasciviousness. Nikolai had managed to read something about it in a couple of magazines, but in principle he was still a virgin, in spite of his mature age, and therefore he was now extremely nervous. Being a sensitive, shy and inexperienced boy inside, to the outside world he had long ago projected the image not of a boy, but that of a man, both experienced and reasonable and even Mira flatly refused to believe that she was his first woman.

"How will Mira think of me, once all my inexperience becomes evident? Why would she baby sit me?" Nikolai was thinking, as the tram trembled. Strangely this trembling of the tram, did not create the usual reaction in his pants, and he began to get upset with this omen.

Mira of course had told him that she was not interested in the physical aspect of love, and that she was swept away by his voice, that she was interested in their conversations; however, it turned out recently that all they were interested in was to roam around the city and to kiss endlessly without saying a word. They had found their favorite sites at the Petrograd Side, on Vasilyevsky Island, near Isakovsky square, at the Nikola's, on the banks of the Priazhka river, in the curves of the Kryukov canal, and on the banks of the Fontanka... Nikolai managed to put his hand under Mira's clothes several times, and he was amazed by the velvet texture of her skin that was hidden from the outside world; but weather was bad, and a space suit of sweaters, coats, and scarves chained desires of their hearts.

"I cannot handle myself, I am only human. What can I do? One day the act of love will turn into the same routine for me as that of reading in English," Nikolai studied this language on his own in order to be able to read some of the philosophers in the original. "Some time ago the language seemed to me to be unknown, strange, and invincible; but now I subconsciously swallow entire lines. It is so great that in the study of English I am not necessarily dependent on other people. I learned it from books, and no one observed my weakness. With love it is more complex...

But I am a reasonable person. I should somehow calm down. It is necessary to find some solution, tactics in the case of failure… Let us imagine if she would not forgive me… That would mean that she is not worth loving… This is nonsense. She is my whole cosmos! She is unique in her kind. I have never had and never will again have this chance. Such women do not usually give me even the slightest bit of attention. I got lucky. Circumstances were so randomly formed in such a way that Mira fell into this illusion, as if it were precisely me whom she needs at this moment. And most of all I fear, that this illusion will be shattered today. Sex is a very dangerous check on the relationships, especially those that are not built on sex… So it seems me. Maybe I should wait? Not to hurry? No… I will not miss this chance…"

When he saw Mira in the cloakroom, Nikolai immediately stammered; but decisively he declared that they should forget about the lectures and go to Mikhail's place. Her face became so gloomy, that it frightened him.

"We should talk…" she said seriously. "Let us go somewhere…"

They left the university and hid in the first alleyway.

"Mira, Mirochka… I wanted to tell you… I wanted to tell you that I want it to last forever… I would not be able to survive if I lose you… You… Please stay with me forever…" Nikolai spoke as if the words were flying out of his mouth, short of breath because of what could come next.

"I have to apologize to you," Mira also said hastily.

"For what?" I need you for the rest of my life... Yes, forever... What apology? Why?"

"I acted as if I lost my mind. I have drawn you into this hopeless relationship."

"I love you! What are you talking about?" Nikolai almost screamed breathlessly.

"Quiet! Someone might hear us... I love you too, but nothing can be done. I am married. I have a small child. I do not want to hurt them. Our romance went too far..."

"What happened?"

"I am afraid..."

"Of what? Maybe I was too hasty about this stupid key?"

"I am afraid that this key embodies all of your intentions... I am afraid that this is all that you are thinking about."

"You... You..."

"I am another one of your girls that you will enjoy and throw away… and I would have no place to go after that, only to kill myself…"

"What the hell are you talking about! I have not even thought about it… I mean, don't think that I…"

"This is exactly what I mean, and I am right."

"You are not the 'next one'… You are unique!"

"It does not matter. I was not looking for love when I met you."

"Not looking for love?"

"Well, I mean, not physical love… But you are interested exactly in this side of love… I was looking for understanding; I was looking for a soul mate…"

"And you haven't found a soul mate?"

"I found one, but this soul doesn't think of anything except about the commonplace mattress…"

"That's stupid, it's not true!"

"I know men too well… When your stare becomes hard and focused, then I know exactly what you are thinking about…"

"But am I not human after all? I am not an angel without a body… I am just a simple human, Mira!"

"Well, you know, that's not enough for me…"

"Are you looking for an angel?"

"I am looking for love… Not physical pleasures, but for love in its broad universal meaning… I am sorry… I feel as if I have a fever… Forgive me for the love of God. There are so many loose women who are much more attractive than me… Just don't pick on me… Please! Let me go… Why do you need me! Let me go! Do you hear me? I beg you!"

Mira's face pinched in and tears poured down her reddening cheeks. Sobbing, she muttered inaudibly and dimly:

"So if you want I could introduce you to one of my friends? She doesn't care… You will like here! Honestly!"

"What are you talking about! I even… I have not even thought about it…" Nikolai tried to lie, but then understood that it would be fake and stupid to do so. "Yes, you are right… I am thinking only about that. I am a low-life. I do not deserve you…"

"That's beside the point! Deserve, not deserve… You are speaking as if you were at a Party meeting… Let us forget about what happened between the two of us … Let us forgive each other… Forgive me, because I was looking in you for something impossible, and found an average man…. And you were looking for a woman in me and found… an average idiot! An idiotic peasant girl which our brain-damaged city is full of…"

"What the hell is this! You completely misunderstood me… I did not have you in mind…" Nikolai clenched his head and he began to sway it from side to side… "What can I do? How can I explain … You see right through me … But I am not like that, I am not like that… Yes, I lost my mind, you drove me out of my mind… I could not even imagine that a woman could be so attractive… I always despised the physical aspect, I thought that it was nonsense, ashes, nothing… Yes, precisely, something negligible and insignificant. In any case, it is not worthy of this stress in mind and emotions…"

"You don't know me at all…" continued Mira.

"I adore you!"

"You fantasize about some desirable idol, but in reality I am completely different…"

"Yes, I fantasize about you being naked all the time, obsessively thinking about how you look underneath…"

"So you see… and I feel that. I can not give this to you… I am not in this state of mind…"

"But I do not need anything anymore… Let us just be friends, stroll in the streets, and hold each other by the hands… Talk…"

"Yes, I always admitted that your voice charms me, but sometimes you say such things that make me want to cry. Sometimes I am simply in despair because of how distant we are from each other…"

"Like how?"

"I love our city, but you deeply despise it…"

"That's silly… I also love it. What other city should I love?.. But the city is beside the point… Why do I deserve it?"

"See that's what I mean… 'Why do I deserve it?..' And me? What about how I feel? You are too focused on yourself…"

"Oh for God's sake… Mira… All I wanted… Yes, I am not a monk… Yes, I want you. Yes and this desire is burning me from inside and I cannot rest in peace…" he said in a voice short of breath, as if he flew from the bridge into the Neva river and was drowning…

"Are you crying?"

"No, there is just something in my eye… and it's hard for me to breathe…"

"That's OK. It is better than when a speck of dust gets in your soul… You are crying…"

"No."

"I see it for myself… You know what? It is not working out very well… Let's go to your Mikhail… Only promise me that you won't make a pass at me. OK? Let's sit quietly. Talk like human beings. Don't cry or I will also cry..."

"I am not crying…" said Nikolai as he wiped his eyes.

η

Mikhail lived in Tuchkov alley with a gloomy enclosed courtyard. As they entered the apartment, they unexpectedly ran into the owner who was tinkering around with some rags, and was covered in paint…

"Don't pay any attention to me… Pretend that that I'm not here," said Mikhail.

With a reproachful and despairing glance, Nikolai said, "And you call yourself my friend… It is already 11 o'clock, and you are still home…"

"I am leaving already, don't worry… I just thought you wouldn't come…"

Mikhail scanned Mira from her head to her toes, and then again from bottom to top; then he turned and trudged away in a dignified and deliberately slow pace. Mira followed the steps of the hairy genius with a heavy unblinking stare.

"And now he's going to think that something's going on between us… What if he knows someone who knows my husband?

"Then we will be hurting for nothing… I promised that I wouldn't come on to you…"

"It doesn't matter any more. What do you mean 'for nothing'? The unfaithfulness is obvious; there is no doubt about it… I can't think of anyone else except you. I almost called my husband your name a few times…"

"Really?" Nikolai brightened up. "I also think about you all the time, how you look…"

"Naked?"

"No…"

"Hey, don't lie… You are always stripping me down with your eyes…"

"Well then… yes…"

"So, if you think it's so important…" said Mira as she slowly started taking off her sweater. Nikolai wanted to stop her, and say that she had misunderstood him; but he could not. He got short of breath and simply settled down on a chair while staring at her.

She started to unbutton her blouse while keeping her gaze fixed on Nikolai. It seemed to him that her eyes were brimming with tears, but he said nothing. For in the last few days he had been obsessed with this body, entranced really, and was ready to do anything to finally view the object of his desire.

Underneath her blouse there appeared a bra of an expectedly bright hue of red. It was as if Mira, when dressing this morning, had wanted to protect herself from possible encroachments. The color of red symbolizes danger, even though there are those that may become aroused by the sight of it such as bulls at a bullfight, or incite one to a sudden aggression…

Nikolai looked at Mira's suddenly bare stomach, and it seemed to him to be as that of a child. For some reason he imagined a children's clinic and envisioned a kindly doctor who would enter and start to feel her stomach. Nikolai wanted to pass on this image to Mira, but he was afraid to breath a word and in so doing spook Mira into changing her mind.

Mira was stunningly beautiful even in this silly half-naked condition. But as soon as she unlatched her bra and threw it to the side, Nikolai's head began to spin. Two small vulnerable breasts jutted outwards, away from each other.

Her nipples turned out be to tiny, bright pink and charmingly pointing out of her rounded ovals like the points of the onion domes over churches.

"So that's what they are like…" broke out Nikolai.

"Like what?" asked Mira quietly.

"Vulnerable…"

"That's what I say…" signed Mira.

Nikolai did not notice that Mira had now discarded the rest of her clothes, remaining in her tiny panties, which seem to have also been chosen subconsciously that morning along with the bra. Her body was well-proportioned. There was nothing in her shape that could be wrong. Her legs were smooth and shapely. Above it all, Nikolai was most impressed by her knees. Just like her stomach, they looked completely girlish.

One more slight gesture and now Mira was completely naked. She crossed her legs so that her private place was now totally concealed by the triangle between her thighs; she clenched her fists at her sides and started to peer around self-consciously.

"Can I dress now?" she said after pause, in a slightly teasing manner.

It seemed that she was waiting for something from him. At first he wanted to ask for her permission but then understood that words would just spoil everything.

He silently stood up and then – as if admiring a sculpture in the Summer Garden – he slowly circled around Mira without taking his eyes off of her. She continued to look to the side, with her fists still clenched at the sides of her slim body, which caused her muscles to tighten just so, that her back seemed divided into two halves by a spell-binding crease that stretched along her spine and deepened into the tender groove leading to the temple of her ass. Nikolai carefully touched Mira on her back a slight bit below her shoulder blades; and encountering no objections, he began slowly stroking her body with both hands.

"You promised you wouldn't come on to me," Mira whispered almost inaudibly.

"I'm not coming on to you," he replied in a surprisingly low voice, and his hands started to wander caressingly over Mira's back, slowly moving up and down. Then he tenderly kissed Mira on the neck as she sighed. Staying behind her, he started to caress her breasts, which turned out to be surprisingly firm. The nipples were entrapped between his fingers, making the breast shiver; and Nikolai experienced a strange wave of happiness. He stood over Mira and could see over her back, and observed all of her frontal vulnerability. And now he became bolder, and his right hand slipped down over Mira's stomach, gradually inching its way towards the center of the universe – to the alpha and omega of all existence… His left hand remained clutching her breast. When he reached the innermost spot, Mira sighed and leaned her whole body backwards towards him. He could see that she had closed her eyes and was waiting for further decisive actions from him.

With his index finger, Nikolai started to slowly search for her most private of spots; and with this search Mira became even more excited. Finally he found the firm button and started to tenderly pull it from side to side. Mira gave a slight moan and started to collapse, and for just a second he thought that she would fall.

He helped her down to her knees and then carefully stepped around her and faced her from the front. Mira suddenly and hungrily attacked his zipper, pulling it down and extracting the object of his worries earlier that morning. It was in a semi-aroused state, and Nikolai was a bit self-conscious about it; but as soon as Mira took that willful creature into her mouth, it was as if his entire consciousness moved into that trifling branch of his physicality – and subsequently concentrated his entire being into that single point. Mira started to move her head rhythmically, hardly touching the surface of the rigid column with her teeth. Nikolai wanted to close his eyes, but could not stop from watching Mira's head as it rhythmically moved closer to – then further away from his stomach, or from his hand gently holding the back of her head as if it were directing and guiding the pace and depth of the penetration, as well as from her shoulders that seemed surprisingly childish and skeletal. He could not see all of her breasts, only the right nipple which swung in a cadence to the side of the main object of Mira's interest, which had now swollen to such an extent that it barely fit in her month – such that Mira often paused to catch her breath. It seemed as if her cheeks would bulge. But above all he was mesmerized by her ass, seen from above, and the prim heels positioned to the sides of this billowing round crease. Everything that Mira was doing, and the way she looked at this moment, drove Nikolai up into a strange and indescribable state of exaltation. It seemed to him that in front of him was some new, interplanetary creature…

In the meanwhile, Mira – this interplanetary, far-away quintessence – caught her breath and held back her tears and stopped the literally cathartic spasms of sobs which were thoroughly inappropriate for this moment. She felt that Nikolai's obsessed fascination was ordinary for her, but for him was a new and fascinating process – she did not want to spoil this long-awaited happiness for him, understanding and absolving him of his fixation and intoxication. In much the same way we would regard a child, absorbed in his joy of finally receiving a long-desired puppy for which he had been hopelessly pining away for due to his mother's allergy.

And whereupon his mother, having swallowed a veritable cocktail of drugs, is smiling while categorizing in her head all the potential troubles that will inevitably ensue, and looking on at the simple happiness of her child while holding in the bitter tears of tender emotion over his naiveté and her sacrifice for it – keeping silent for as long as possible in order to not spoil the long-awaited joy of her child.

θ

The road rhythmically flowed under the soles of the snugly tied boots. The pebbles, bound to their neighbors – small shadows, distinguished themselves from each other, each in its proper spot. The road dust rose slightly and then immediately subsided, resembling the surface of the moon. It is as if during childhood, deprived of actual amusements, you fly over the surface of the road, carried by the light and not attached to the plodding pace – you imagine yourself as an astronaut intensely seeking a place to land.

The tip of the walking stick, made from a strong piece of bamboo, left behind tiny craters on the desolate surface of the road, and in disturbing the harmony of the chaotic patters of the grains of sand created an even greater feeling of being on the moon.

The gentleman in the grey raincoat was walking without any obvious goal. Nicholas Bang was an eccentric personality and rarely coerced himself into have a walk with a goal in the normal sense of the word. For this purpose he had assistants, attorneys, butlers, cooks... Walks, for him, were a way he could pleasantly dive deep into his thoughts, a world in which he spent the most of his time.

In this forty-year old man it is difficult to recognize Nikolai Bangushin. He has been altered almost completely. Premature grey hair had conspired together with a steadily advancing baldness in what had previously been an unruly clump of hair and now serves as undeniable proof of the ravages of time.

The name had also changed, and with that name an old person had disappeared with a new one appearing in his place. Thus happens to things, such as when an old sofa is sent on it last trip to the dump, while the impressions it has left on the carpet are covered by a new sofa, still innocent, having not yet experienced the delight of our heavy backsides; and so even though the room still contains the nominal essence of the same object – the object is not the same; it has come to replace its faulty predecessor, whose fault was only the weariness of its shabby profile, baldness, sagginess, and the lack of trust in human nature. Sofas know us from such an unexpected perspective that it is difficult to expect extreme loyalty or selfless admiration. They leave our lives lightly, and exactly thus did Nikolai Bangushin when he changed his bodily dwelling – not exactly as a glove, but still without any share of guilt and rarely thinking of the actual process of the developments concerning himself.

Mr. Nicholas Bang had already been living for twenty years away from his land of birth. He could scarcely recall the circumstances that drove him out of Russia at the start of the 90's. Shady business or fraud, simply stated, forced him to leave in such a rush without saying farewell to anybody, with one small suitcase that held more dollars than actual clothes, and to depart for Finland. He did not even time to hide the money, and as they headed towards the border, while the other passengers went to smoke in the vestibule area, he feverishly wrapped his undisguised capital into a newspaper and stashed it into a small compartment in the luggage shelf of the carriage.

How such a philosophically oriented boy got himself into such a financial scheme, it is hard to say, except that in those years everyone seemed to lose his mind, and after the both of his partners were killed by the bullets of their rivals, he had no choice but to take their collective capital, and buy a tourist trip to Finland with no intention of ever coming back.

He had left during the first year of the university, but Nikolai did not really regret it. Philosophy in its academic form gave him a strong feeling of nausea. What really tormented him, however, was that he had left Mira behind in Russia, as she had become very close to him during the preceding half year and he could not imagine life without her.

On the evening of his departure he telephoned her without caring whether her husband picked up the phone. Mira immediately arrived at their cherished place, where they had previously spent a long stream of delightful hours. After having heard the muddled explanations of Nikolai, she cried; and then when he held out the packet of dollars, she threw it on the floor.

"You don't understand… I am going to be waiting for you… You need this money so that you can come…"

"It's all over," sobbed Mira.

"No! No! No!" Nikolai hissed in frenzy.

The distant scene came to the mind of the gentleman in the grey raincoat without any external cause; maybe some complex association appeared in his head as a result of seeing the pebbles on the moon-like road, and the resulting memory suddenly surfaced from the depths with his ancient and desperate "No! No! No!"

"Why am I alone? Why all this moon dust, this wilderness, this loneliness?..."

In academic circles Nicholas Bang was known as an unsentimental being. If by chance one of his many opponents were to see his silhouette on the road to the manor in Cambridge, he would think to himself that this scoundrel is again plotting some new scheme;

while one of his all too few admirers would think that Mr. Bang is pondering over one of his upcoming philosophical concepts. But it would have been impossible to guess that the thoughts of this cold man were focused on the feelings he had left behind in St. Petersburg in the distant past.

Mr. Bang had quite a scandalous reputation. Having appeared in Cambridge a couple of decades ago literally out of nowhere, he had successfully studied philosophy for several years; but when he worked on his doctorate he got into such conflict with everyone that the dons at Cambridge, normally quite moderate in their bitchiness, and quite without conspiracy, obstructed him at every turn and would in no way award him his doctorate in philosophy. As a matter of fact the scandals surrounding Mr. Bang arose not only and not so much because of his prickly character, but rather due to his manner of questioning everything and everybody, as if he were a modern-day Socrates or Descartes. He would not accept the foundations of modern science, saying the academic circus was leading not to the future, but following the witch-hunting tenets of the past; and his heretical statements that the foundations of scientific approach required updating could not be accepted by even the most moderate and democratic of the professors. They were especially offended by the fact that the arguments provided by Mr. Bang were quite substantial and were originated from the field of philosophical argument from whence come all bone-crushing criticisms of our world… These arguments were based on the limited nature of human reasoning, on the illusory nature of our world, and on the eternal effort of the scholars of all times and peoples to establish themselves as the benchmark for all matters.

His opponents considered him to be a knave, a rogue, and a rich Neanderthal, even though they recognized that in his rough manner of arguing the facts, there were elements of a rational person still at the earliest stages of development. After one of Bang's articles was published in an improbable manner in a prestigious journal only after a low-key, viperous battle, it became clear the life in academic circles would not be for him. Three times his doctoral thesis was sent up for revision, and when for a further petty objection his defense was failed again, which is quite uncommon for the British academic dons, Bang did the unthinkable – he left the university in a demonstrable manner. But, the joy of his unwitting inquisitors was to be short-lived.

Mr. Bang had always been involved in financial gambles all his life. By the end of the 90's his capital had grown, like bread rising in the oven, because he had created an Internet site of questions and answers to eternal questions, that became so popular with students all around the world, that the number of people visiting the site was comparable to that of the leading porno sites of the day. The constant updating of the site, with its transformation into an enormous megalopolis of blogs, individual web pages, where people began to express their opinions, brought him even more popularity.

Before the Dot-com crash Bang managed to sell his site at a tremendous profit to a leading American telecommunications company. Then, he did not indulge in luxury but immediately invested almost all of his gains into the shares of oil production companies at the time when the price of oil was at $ 10 per barrel; then ten years later, when the prices jumped up to $ 100 per barrel, Bang suddenly became a multimillionaire. So, what did the oil magnate do when his doctoral dissertation was rejected yet another time? He declared war on his own university. This was a full-on war with multi-dimensional attacks and feigned retreats. After spending more than fifteen years on his studies, Bang did not ready to give up. There was a reason, after all, that he changed his gentle name of Bangushin to the sharp English word of "Bang", which means "explosion". He was actually very much like dynamite. Several of his enemy-professors ingloriously added heart attacks to their service records, and the department started to lose its reputation, as Bang was never stingy in the continued massive attack against his Alma Mater, using all types of media and the Internet. In the end, Mr. Bang was suddenly notified that he was awarded the doctorate degree; but it was absolutely clear that he would never again be welcome in academic circles.

However Bang was not silenced by this and continued his more then uncommon activities. It seemed that this person had set as his objective in life to discredit the modern academic world. At first the modern-day Socrates was ignored out of contempt. Then he was laughed at. When it became clear that each mockery came at a dear cost to those who mocked him, academic society began to ignore him, but, at this point out of fear of meddling with him…In the meantime it was difficult not to notice the activities of Bang. Through anonymous funds and organizations he was able to draw the best scientists under his wing, and reward them so well that many of them started to support him, putting their academic reputations at risk. Bang most of all liked to surround himself with those who had been wronged by official academia; within only five years he had created an entire alternative empire consisting of research institutes, academic journals, and even educational institutions. It was true that his request to receive a royal charter from Her Majesty, the Queen, to establish a new university in Great Britain was denied. But one should give Mr. Bang credit where it is due: he restrained himself from bringing the Queen to court, although this did not happen in so far as it was impossible, but rather because in her denial Her Majesty had contained the temporizing word "yet", and thus there was still a hope that her Royal Opinion would change. Despite that, during an interview in the Sun paper, Bang had joked that if started to question the legitimacy of the British monarchy then he could possibly immediately receive the royal charter to found the university. He got away with this bold move as well.

How did this gentleman "road warrior" differ from any other charlatan creating a new sect? Mainly because he did not propose anything; he did not have new theories; he only criticized the old ones and demanded a review of their foundations. The actions of Bang were therefore so invulnerable precisely because his criticism was extremely valid. Scientists and philosophers are well aware of these arguments; but either they tried to stay silent about them or simply overlooked them. What else would you expect? Should one just go hide at home? As with all naïve idealists, Bang was a nuisance to just about everyone. He thrust his nose not only into philosophy, but also criticized the methodology used in history, psychology, sociology, and even cosmology did not escape from his crushing criticism. It seemed that this person was out to change the way all mankind was thinking.

The tabloids willingly supported the uproar around each succeeding scandal brought on by Bang. Thus far it was a fact that politicians had remained neutral towards this "terminator", since for them the old university system was like a small chicken bone stuck in their throats. They regarded the universities as having sucked out and squandered public funds, issuing heaps of senseless scientific articles and good-for-nothing graduates with magnificent-sounding diplomas.

The most incomprehensible issue for the opponents of Bang was the fact that he did not seem to draw any tangible benefits from his activities. His books were badly sold. They were written in a dry scientific language and did not inspire interest amongst the general public; and of course scientists did not buy the books out of principle. Bang was only incurring losses in dispensing his capital out to various alternative scientific projects and publications. Being an overly trusting man, he frequently fell victim to cheats who tried to take advantage of him; yet his naïveté was accompanied by such an elaborate and burning vindictiveness that many preferred to let him be.

Why did Bang's walk along the path leading to the manor dredge up such a strange recollection? Was it possible that Bang was not happy? Maybe he wanted to have children, comfort, and a warm home? He did not want to buy a house, but renting one was inconvenient, so it was necessary to spend a part of his investment in the oil company stocks to use for the purchase of home for himself. Nicholas did not believe in private property. Like any philosopher he was aware that we all stay in this world for only an insignificant period of time, and therefore the accumulation of property is meaningless, naïve, and freezes liquid capital which could be used for more refined purposes, such as to the continued vexation of the academic community, or the tapping of funds for the global energy shortage.

The huge manor satisfied his ambitions. But apart from himself, no one else lived there. In the 90's Bang had married and spent a few years with an acrid Brit; but it was not clear whether this marriage had been made in order to obtain a British residency permit, or whether it had some genuine sentimental aspect.

After Bang had parted with his wife, he had several short-term affairs; but due to his complex nature and the nature of his business, those affairs quickly died out. Despite that he was no monk. About once a week he would use call girls, preferring those who only understood English with difficulty, and even then did not let them stay the night.

The villages besides which Mr. Bang lived were called Kirtling and Upend. From the 16th to the 19th centuries Kirtling was known by the name of Catlidge, and the village of Upend had been known as Upheme, which in old English means "upper dwelling". These two villages were comfortably situated in the eastern part of the County of Cambridge, on the border of the County of Suffolk, five miles to the south of Newmarket town.

Bang slowly approached the gates to his manor. Of course, one person does not need an entire manor to himself, so of course his ambition must have driven him. One way or another, it was a manor that was bought.

The first time Kirtling was mentioned was in the year 1219. Later references indicate that it had a moat crossed by a bridge in 1260. By the 15th century the manor consisted of the hall, kitchen, and a chapel. In 1424 a new hall was built for the earl of Warwick using 100 oaks from Kirtling park.

In the year 1537 Lord Edward North reconstructed the manor all over again. A new hall was built along with new towers around the three-storied building over the gates. By 1660 the Kirtling castle was the biggest building in Cambridgeshire. The Norths were actively involved in politics. Edward North was a close advisor to King Henry VIII. The second Lord North, Roger, lived in grand style. He had a cook, gardener, shoemaker, doctor, horseman, secretary and even a jester.

In essence, except for a shoemaker and a doctor, Mr. Bang had a household similar to that of Lord Roger North. He also had horses; and the roles of a cook and jester were combined in one person. Nicholas had ordered a cook from Italy and this magician of saucepans and ladles had a funny last name: Beer. Yes, exactly Senor Giovanni Beer. Mr. Bang was obsessed about this linguistic coincidence.

The third and the fourth Lord Norths had a hunting park which was well stocked with deer. At the end of the 17th century the castle slid into the state of neglect. In 1801 the larger part of it was demolished. Today only the famous towers and the three-story building over the gates remain standing from ancient times.

In 1827 Maria North set about restoring her ancestral estate inheriting it from her eccentric uncle who had joined Greek Orthodox Church and founded his own university on the island of

Corfu. Thus Mr. Bang was not the first inhabitant of the castle who had aspired to found his own university.

Having purchased the manor, Bang embarked on an expensive renovation program, and being a true perfectionist he turned the shabby building into the epitome of modern elegance. Only the walls from the old building were left alone, all the rest was altered and eviscerated in accordance with his taste. It seemed that, together with the shreds of old wallpaper and the remnants of dilapidated sofas, the ghosts had also left the castle.

Having entered the big dinner hall Bang absent-mindedly looked at the newly rebuilt fireplace and headed for the kitchen where his only constant companion, Giovanni Beer, was working.

"How was your walk, Sir?" cheerfully asked the cook. "I made you hot soup. I always make soup when it is cloudy outside and you go for a walk…Who knew that you would be back before it started…"

"What started?" Nicholas asked absent-mindedly, having been shaken up by the chatter coming with an Italian accent. Bang had acquired a Pavlovian response – in his mind the cook's voice was associated with eating.

"Oh yes, yes… that it would rain today…"

"For England that would be quite a rare event…" snapped Mr. Bang. "I am hungry... What else do we have today besides soup?"

"Today being Friday, as always, I have obtained three dozen of the freshest oysters… Sir, would you like me to open a bottle of champagne? For the main course – Beef Wellington, and for dessert, banana cake."

"Excellent… I am going to rest a bit. Sound the gong when it is done…"

"Certainly, sir," Giovanni smiled in a friendly and slightly subservient manner.

Nicholas very much treasured the skills of his cook as well as his ability in the event of any sadness to cheer him up. Every morning at 10 o'clock for breakfast and at four o'clock for dinner Giovanni would bang the huge gong in the dining room.

Bang dined surrounded by his few servants. To the right of him he positioned Giovanni, to the left – his workers, who were always building and rebuilding something in the manor. At the other end of the big table usually sat the cleaning lady, Maggie, the housekeeper, Sandra and his personal assistant, Mr. Lockhart.

Strangely enough Bang enjoyed this company. The conversation at dinner was simple, and the rude jokes of Giovanni entertained the diners; and so, Bang was content and joyful. It seemed as if these people were his family. Bang did not keep in close touch with his parents who were still living in Russia. He would send them abundant financial support and call them roughly twice a month. However, he cared about the people at the table as if they were his relatives and knew all their family members by name, and always made an effort to solve their simple problems. Bang treated them as equals and did not expect either gratitude or special respect towards him. In return they provided tolerable service and even some illusion of loyalty.

These people were friendly and simple-minded; they did not argue about philosophy with him, and it is supposed that they would gladly beat up his rivals, if they dared to show up at the doorsteps of his manor.

ι

You could not say that Bang did not have any visitors. Recently when his contra-scientific empire became stronger, other people began to show their interest towards him. Bang invited them in selectively, but one way or another almost every day someone would appear at the manor after dinner. Nickolas invited only those who he thought would be interesting to him. And today it was a professor from Cambridge that had a similar reputation of being an obnoxious critic of modern science who had come over.

The partners in conversation settled in chairs in a cozy study room with book shelves rising to the ceiling and two rich Gobelin tapestries and smoked cigars. After some ordinary insignificant chatter a talk in the style of forgotten dialogues of Plato emerged.

"You, Dr. Bang, believe that only to you has the truth been revealed," rumbled the professor laughingly and in a friendly manner. "And so, what do you consider to be truth? How do you know for sure that you have indeed discovered truth? Is it even possible to find truth at all?"

"But, of course, the crux of the matter is how you define truth," answered Nicholas as he also smiled in his turn.

The professor was silent. He was studying the statuettes scattered all over Bang's study room. A Hermes statute tens feet tall was standing proudly on the desk. A muscular Hercules was positioned on a book case. And nearby, Themis – the Greek goddess of Justice, standing over an exiled and gloomy Napoleon with a cannon ball tied to his foot were on the book shelves.

"What an interesting choice of bronze figures," said the professor.

"Now I thought that you were talking about the truth. How true is it really – what you have just said?"

"I think it was quite true… What could be wrong about what I have said about your bronze figures?"

"It's only that they are not bronze. They are made out of a special rubber…"

"Really! It is not possible! May I?" The professor stood up and took the statuette of Hermes into his hands. It was much lighter than it would have been if it was made of bronze, but the external similarity was absolute.

"So, you see, professor, your senses and experiences have fooled you. Therefore, what is, in your opinion, the truth?"

"Usually the truth is defined as a correlation between the statement or perception and some criteria of truthfulness," said the professor absent-mindedly as he placed the statuette back.

"Well, the different types of truth are distinguished from each other, not with out reason," said Bang.

"And here I had thought that there should only be one truth," smiled the professor.

"Any truth is relative... I would not give a definition of truth, without taking into account its relativity. The relativity is also, of course, an illusion. But the absolute truth is probably more of an illusion than relative truth. A truth that most of the universe will not be able to challenge is most probably nonsense. The absolute truth is unreachable and every rational argument is impossible without a dose of agnosticism and skepticism…"

Bang was bored, but he hoped that sooner or later the conversation would go in a direction that would be interesting for him.

"Therefore, speaking in simple terms, it is possible to only approach the truth, yet never to reach it?"

"Yes, but in the process of this approach, new assumptions are being created and old ones are being discarded. This process embodies the main principle of the human cognition, as well as – you can say – progress. And, I do not want to be deprived of this process by having returned to this simplistic and reductionist statement that 'we can only say that we do not know anything'. So then, after this, what comes next? Let's go back to the trees? To ignorance? To darkness?" the professor became agitated.

"Lord no! I am not trying to deprive mankind of the right to seek truth. Furthermore, there should be, at least theoretically, an undeniable, constant, once – and – for – all established knowledge. Some kind of *absolute* truth. Let's imagine that we agree that even though absolute truth is not reachable, the idea of absolute truth still exists. Therefore, if the idea exists, then absolute truth should exist as well…Even though it might be out of reach for a human brain, or even though no one at all can comprehend it. But the term exists. The definition is reached. Thus, absolute truth does exist, does not it? Moreover, "relative truth" is not a very appropriate term. "Partial truth" would be a more precise term," Bang now began to get more involved.

"I think that the concept of absolute truth is extremely important as a guiding star. Even though it might be imaginary, it would still lead us in the right direction…" a slight interest appeared in the astigmatic eyes of the professor which were framed by thick glasses.

"Then why would you need that?" Bang asked suddenly. "Let's assume that some absolute truth does exist. And yet it is not attainable by anyone. Then, how could it be a guiding star? And if not, then what would be the meaning of its existence? We, the people, are just computers. Although we might have feelings, sensations… we are in essence, just dolls, mechanisms for the input and output of information. Why would we need absolute truth? For example, let's take analytical truth, wherein the property that is assigned to the object is contained in the definition itself.

Or synthetic truth, wherein the inclusion of this property requires the introduction of additional information. Those are operational types of truth, which are convenient to use. This discourse about absolute truth, on the other hand, might be entertaining, but unfortunately, quite useless."

"So, you propose to measure the concepts based on their usefulness and cast away those that you do not see as being useful or useful *yet* from the conventional point of view?" objected the professor.

"Well, it was not I who set up these barriers," said Bang cunningly. "For example, take the term '*mericsumus*'."

"Excuse me? What is that?" the professor was at a loss.

"Oh, it's nothing. It is just a word I have invented. But if one were to follow your logic, since I have created it – it exists...Would you like me to define it? It would be my pleasure..."

"Ok, ok, don't bother... it would be quite meaningless..."

"So, it would be meaningless in the same way that would apply to the statement that 'if absolute truth has a definition, then it exists'. In this case, we run into the concept of "existence"... Shady business... "Existence" cannot be separated from reality, and reality is a product of what can be perceived by our senses, and our consciousness... Thus, it would be logical to consider what does not exist or what does exist, but we do not know about its existence, as not existing."

"Would you not agree that the concept of truth is important enough that we must define it precisely?"

"That would be difficult not to agree with," agreed Mr. Bang

"So then let us assume that the truth is a certain characteristic that defines the degree of perfection of thought or statement allowing for its categorizing as cognition or knowledge," recited the professor as if in a rote manner.

"And in which dictionary of philosophy did you find this definition?" mocked Mr. Bang'

"Why, are you not satisfied by this definition? And, I write these definitions myself…" answered the professor in an irritated manner.

"No, it does not satisfy me at all," said Bang sharply.

"Why not?"

"You are trying to offer an answer to a problem in which all the variables are not known."

"Why do you think so?"

"See for yourself… "Perfection of thought." But to define "perfection" we need to know the definition of "truth." Do you see what the problem is? You can't define an unknown variable by using another unknown concept…"

"The closer something is to the truth, the more perfect it is..." stated the professor falteringly.

"That's just it...words, words, words... But the meaning is not clear. And then, I believe that you also mentioned "knowledge". So, what is knowledge if is not something approaching the truth? Therefore, it is clear that your definition, even though seemingly well put together and standard, does not hold water...It is the same as if I would have defined my *meriksumus* using some *summerikus*... Does this help you?"

"But then, you would again deprive mankind of the opportunity to define the most basic concepts," contradicted the professor as he started examining the rows of books. There were books everywhere in the Bang's study. Here he mostly kept his collections of encyclopedias. In addition to the book case containing the first edition of the Encyclopedia Britannica dated at the end of the 18th century as well as the more relatively recent 1999 edition in 33 volumes, the study was filled with book shelves of French and German encyclopedias.

"How is this so? The definition becomes feasible if one introduces the necessary stipulations..." Mr. Bang revived the conversation.

"Well, let's make it simpler... Truth we can define as knowledge (the very meaning of knowledge) or the recognized reality. The opposites of truth are the concepts of lie and fallacy," said the Professor thoughtfully.

"And yet again we are not getting anywhere…" smiled Bang.

"I think I am beginning to understand… I believe I know what definition would satisfy you…" the professor said suddenly.

"Really?"

"Yes… What if I add the following stipulation: Truth in the human perception…?"

"You are absolutely right…" rejoiced Bang. "However, let me try… Truth, in the human perception, is knowledge, by this meaning some information acquired at a certain moment in the development of a person, group of people or by mankind in general – information that is manifested by the consistency of conclusions based on the analyses of impulses from senses or internal impulses originated in the human brain. Having compared these individual conclusions with the conclusions made by other people, a person can perceive the knowledge about a phenomenon or object as being truthful or false."

"Then based on your definition, if we see that the sun sets into the ocean, then it must be true…" the professor would not be calm.

"Certainly…" Bang suddenly agreed. "Up to the moment that your ears do not hear or your eyes do not read that other people who have the same senses but are also equipped with a more advanced technology state that what you saw – the setting of the sun into the sea – was a fallacy and illusion… There is your concept, which is opposite to truth – lie and fallacy. All definitions should be based on a human being, on his senses and the cognitive process. Otherwise, we would risk roaming round about all the time as has been the case with philosophy for thousands of years. "

"But it seems that your stipulations are implied anyway?"

"My dear professor… It is just as well that… Even though it is not like that at all. A human being is inclined to forget the relativity of his point of view…"

"Indeed, we do not want another point of view… It is far better to say that there is no proof than there exists an alternative point of view…" the professor objected again.

"This is exactly the root of the problem…" smiled Bang in a cunning fashion. "If you find a wallet, but its lawful owner is not around, it does not mean that the wallet is yours. The definition of truth without the stated stipulations is used as a general category, for instance, as a religious, philosophical, scientific, and logical concept. There is a variety of truth criteria in sciences and philosophy. In logic where truth is one of the major subjects of examination, the criteria of truth include consistency and logical validity. In some religions the criterion of truth is divine revelation…. And this is not that far from burning heretics at the stake…"

"And in such a way you easily discard Kant's "things in themselves," the view of things and phenomena beyond our senses?" clarified the professor gloomily.

"How do I do that? I look at the world as a "thing in itself" with some of its parts available for our analysis. Kant was too radical for his time, and I am too modest for mine… In general one has to be very careful particularly with definitions of main concepts. It is like when you make a mistake at the beginning of the journey and as a result you end up in the wrong place. Principal definitions are like the beginning of the journey," Bang grew bored once again.

"It is necessary to admit that Parmenides, who was one of the first or at least, as you like to say, 'to the extent that we know of', introduced the philosophical notion of truth. He used it as the antithesis to 'opinion'. Therefore, constancy is recognized as the main criterion of truth," continued the professor.

"Admirable conservativeness… However, to depend upon constancy is not reliable. We can observe constancy only in the past. We do not know if our constancy will still be a constant in the future. A storm is most likely to erupt after a long period of quiet! The classic definition of truth is quite superficial, but represents the most widespread and accepted concept of truth. This explanation was accepted by many philosophers in different times. This concept is referred to as the classical concept of truth. At first it was formulated by Aristotle. Its essence boils down to the formula 'Truth is the conformity of object and intellect…' In Latin, it might sound like 'Veritas est adaequatio rei et intellectus'. I am sorry… I am not very fluent in Greek. More precisely one can say that 'Truth is the adequate information about an object received via sensual and intellectual comprehension and is characterized based on its reliability.' A different, simpler interpretation is that 'Truth is the adequate reflection of reality in consciousnesses."

"But this does not contradict your definition with stipulations…"

"Yes, but it does not take into account the human element. Truth based on the reflection of an illusionary reality is taken as an absolute by man. Some other theoretical sciences are built around this absolute, as a result of course, we have total nonsense.

"So, do you have anything new to suggest?" the professor would not stop.

"Lord knows, I do not offer anything new. The comprehension of truth as the conformity of objects and knowledge was accepted in the old days by Democritus, Epicurus, and Lucretius. The classical concept of truth was adopted by giants of thought such as Aristotle, ***Foma Akvinsky, Holbach,*** Hegel, and even Marx. The classical concept is intrinsic to the philosophers of the 20th century and many current philosophers. This understanding of truth was characteristic of, for example, English and French philosophers-materialists of the New Age. They defined truth quite clearly by incorporating it into their formulas as the 'adequate reflection of reality', which made them adherents of the classical concept. Materialists quite frequently considered truth to be self-obvious in the sense of rationalistic intuition."

Bang wanted to finish the conversation as soon as possible. To be honest, he was getting sleepy but he intended to invite a girl over. Friday was the best day, because after recharging himself Bang could dedicate the weekend to quiet philosophizing.

"What do you think about the idealistic theory of truth in the ancient tradition of philosophy?"

Bang thought that he did not want to talk about it at all, but still he replied:

"Do you mean Plato, according to whom the truth is the eternal idea as well as other characteristics of other 'ideas' that are beyond time? Well, to repeat myself…Let's imagine that it is so. Let's imagine that these eternal ideas do indeed exist. However, they do really seem to be the fruit of the human consciousness. And as a result – they are just words… Nothing more. Beautiful words… But, they do not have a practical sense even taking into account their universal importance. And it does not matter how many times we reiterate ***Foma Akvinsky who interpreted Aristotle from the idealistic perspective or Augustine who relied on the convictions of Plato who preached the teaching of the inherent nature of true concepts and assertions – this does not change anything. And the fact that Descartes and even Hegel considered the idea as the "truth in itself and for itself" simply proves my doubt... We are born; we live and die in the framework of our human perception and cognition... We consider ourselves being the measure of all things, even those things whose understanding is beyond our grasp...***"

"In this case you would deny the irrational approach to the understanding of truth."

"Existentialists contrasted objective truth with the concept of personal truth, which intuitively perceives the objective reality. Since these considerations help us exist, they are useful for us, but they do not have any independent value."

"Kindly allow me to disagree... Doesn't this mean that you undervalue the level of human knowledge?"

"That would be pointless... Self-depreciation leads nowhere, it, on the other hand, does impede the realistic perception of the world to the same extent as does self-absorption."

Bang stood up and the professor understood that the conversation had reached an end.

ϰ

Having seen off the boring professor Bang checked if the staff had already left for the weekend and that he was alone in the castle. "I live some sort of animal's life," the thought struck him while he was dialing. He used the services of practically all the agencies that provided call-girls; and was so afraid to get attached to even them that he always demanded different women. Since their available number was still limited he sometimes had to share the evening with a woman he had already previously met. However, Bang did not insist on much variation in bed and the women were instructed beforehand about his specific needs and wants, and that he did not like to talk.

This time around Bang opened the door to a blonde woman. Her facial features revealed her to be of Eastern-European origin. For his own specific reasons, Bang preferred exactly this type of women.

"Possibly a Czech or Polish girl… New…" thought Bang to himself in a contented way.

He led his guest into the spacious sitting room, turned on some music and reclined lazily in his armchair. The girl stepped aside a few steps and started to move slowly following the rhythm of the simple melody. Quite quickly she undressed and started to make seductive moves. Bang did not have any concerns about his capabilities since he had recently taken a Viagra so as not to waste the 200 pounds for the next hour and a half.

He closely examined the slim figure of the girl, her slightly large breasts and graceful neck. He adored her legs. Bang summoned the temptress with his finger and let down his guard to vent some steam. By the end the girl began to press and started to feverously scratch his back.

"More! Yes! Yes!" she suddenly screamed…

"Hmm… Russian," thought Bang and came.

He felt surprise and became confused. His guests had never before come so obviously. In such circles losing control was considered to be completely unprofessional and not normal.

"Are you new?" Bang asked in Russian as he handed the strewn-about clothes to the girl.

"Yes…" she answered and lowered her eyes as she did not expect to hear Russian speech coming from a respectable English lord, the resident of a mansion.

"Do not come to me any more," said Bang; paid and abruptly turned her out of doors.

"Jerk," he heard her say from the other side of the door; and he recalled this curse word from childhood that seemed both cute and unsure to Bang. He felt the urge to open the door and call the girl back, but he restrained himself.

"I am a rational man... That is it. It is enough. I do not need other issues or attachments… this is quite enough. I had enough with Mira. And I have had it with others as well. I won't let women turn my brains inside out…"

That night Bang could not sleep. Something kept him from getting into his typical introspective and relaxed mind-set that normally helped him fall asleep. He tried to read, purposely selecting one of the more boring books from his immense library: "Engels and Marx on Religion". This edition was in English, which added even more dryness to the painfully familiar nonsense with rare glimpses of common sense. Finally, at around two in the morning the book fell out of his hands and a light intoxicating dream wrapped around his restless consciousness.

"This is the end!" he heard Mira's voice.

"No! No! No!" shouted Nikolai as he kissed her on her lips, eyes, ears, tasting the bitter salt of Mira's tears on his lips.

"I beg of you… I am pleading with you… stay! I can hide you… Return this cursed money… I will leave my husband… Just do not leave me… Why must you do all this?"

"And really why did I need all this? Mr. Bang sobbed painfully. "Why could not I live a normal human life? Get married to Mira, have children… Why do I need this superiority complex? Living like a solitary bear? What kind of Messiah am I?

In his dream Nikolai did not scream at Mira as happened then, at the real and final farewell. On the contrary, suddenly he eagerly agreed to stay, and she looked straight into his eyes and believed him. Believed him! She showered him with kisses…

"Nikolushka, my darling…"

Mira's body was prim and attractive. And for some reason she looked like the blonde from earlier that evening, but Nikolai did not care. He loved her as he never loved before.

"That dammed pill…" flashed in Bang's mind. It seemed one time was not enough to get all his rocks off.

He felt as if his consciousness was splitting in two. There he was: Nikolai, a boy once again, in love with his precious girl – his tearful and unhappy Mira.

And here is Mr. Bang, who is standing and carefully examining himself and her from all angles, soberly comprehending that there is no way that Mira would still look like that twenty-year old he once knew. So many years have passed!

And it was at this moment that Giovanni came in.

When Mira saw the cook, she rose up, pushed Nikolai away, and immediately merged together with Mr. Bang into one unitary being, as Mira started to hurriedly cover her breasts, which turned out to be the breasts of the blonde from earlier.

"I am mixing up all my women," flashed in the head of Bang.

In the meantime Giovanni was not a bit embarrassed, but rather quickly took off his pants and without paying the least attention to the outraged Bang, started to rape Mira while dirty Italian jests came out of his mouth. She did not resist.

"I like women's flesh," Giovanna kept saying while slowly touching Mira's breasts.

Bang was infuriated. He grabbed a huge kitchen knife, God knows where it came from, and stabbed the cook. Mira looked frightfully at the bloody hands of Bang and whispered to him:

"You will never be happy!"

She said it so clearly and so sharply that Bang woke up immediately. He still heard Mira's voice in his ears. Bang even went

so far as to switch on the lights and look around the room. Of course, it was empty.

His head was wracked with a migraine.

"I must forget you. You probably are not even alive any no longer…" feverishly whispered Bang. Recently he has been talking to himself more and more often, however, mostly in whisper. "Why can you not let me go? When you have abandoned me yourself?"

Again and again Bang recalled the familiar scene down to the very last detail – he remembered all of the details by heart. Mira calmed herself down, took the money for the tickets and said that as soon as she divorced her husband she would come to him… She would follow him anywhere… She would come; he would only have to call for her… "Nikolushka, darling!"

They both were in a hurry; he was late for his train, while she was late for the day care to pick up her son. But as soon as the train began to move, he noticed Mira still on the platform. "She still came by to see me off…" Nikolai opened the window, leaned out, and shouted:

"Mira, everything will be fine! You will come to me, and we will get married!"

The other passengers in the car were laughing in unison; and Mira shrank back, turned away, and slowly left. May be he was mistaken? May be it was not her?

When he was already in Finland, Nikolai put it to her in a question in a letter to her; but, Mira never replied to the question.

What she wrote instead was: "Nikolushka, I have never loved anyone as I have loved you, but I know that I am holding you back... I do not want to be a burden to you. I am leaving you exactly because I really do love you; and you should not argue with me because you also truly love me. Do not write to me anymore. Just remember me."

Strangely the next thing he felt then was a large sense of relief. "Yes, you are right. Everything is extremely complicated. I am a refugee. You are not free…Thank you for everything…"

Then, he sat at his desk and immediately wrote: "Mirchonok, my little bunny… What are you talking about? I will not let you go. I will never betray you. Say 'yes'! And I will turn the whole world upside down. Mira, please be my wife. Do you agree?"

He sent the letter off right away and then waited for an answer. One week passed, then another one, then a third one... It was time to move out of the rented apartment, where he was staying temporarily. He stayed for another month. There still was no answer. And no one answered Mira's phone…

The morning arrived unexpectedly. It was as the light shadow of an early rain sneaked up on you and the feeling of desperation dawned on you quietly – an unnecessary, strange, and inappropriate desperation… When it seemed that all was well, and there was no need for melancholy, and no reasons for this coarse anxiety – nor a heavy apprehension or a dense, primordial feeling, much as a rusty anchor scraping the ocean floor, where knowledge of the inevitability of disappointment spreads to all parts of the consciousness in the morning. Nicholas Bang woke up even though he could not say for sure if he had ever slept at this morning hour.

"It seems I am starting to go insane," he thought with an unexpected sense of relief and quickly jumped out of the bed. His head was spinning and his vision darkened.

"This is nonsense…" whispered Nicholas in a husky voice and having paused indecisively, finally paid attention to his morning ablutions. He suffered from attacks of hypochondria and therefore had already learned not to pay too much attention to his feelings.

A parrot in love

Reads the poems of Petrarch,

Which he heard

Once, on the radio, -

He was muttering as he dressed. The dream still haunted him.

Having dressed neatly, not too pompously, but in a business fashion, Bang stepped down to the study room. Lockhart, his assistant, was waiting for him there; as if something extraordinary had made Mr. Lockhart to come to work on this Saturday morning.

"What has happened?" asked Mr. Bang, repressing his sense of impending doom.

Mr. Lockhart handed the newspaper over to Mr. Bang in silence. The huge headline on the front page stated: "Apologist of Heresy: Parliamentary Investigation of Mr. Bang's Activities."

"I thought that you might need me," the secretary said quietly, and sat on the tail of the guest's chair that was standing next to the owner's desk.

Mr. Bang sat down heavily on the chair and plunged into reading the article. Based on complaints from the three biggest universities in the United Kingdom the Parliamentary Commission had been established to investigate the activities of Mr. Bang. He was accused of the purposeful discrediting of the system of the higher education, falsification of facts and even machination. The article also said that the activities of Mr. Bang were subversion against the interests of the United Kingdom and if his complicity was proven, then he, Bang, would face a long prison term and after which he would have to leave Great Britain. The article finished with an analysis of Bang's work as being "terrorism against British science."

"Well here now I know these scums… These scum that were hiding in the shadows all this time nursing their own bitterness! It could be that they have found their own type in the government, or maybe some member of the Parliament turned out to be someone's gay lover… In this country everything works through one single point… If I only could find out who is behind it all… Mr. Lockhart, if you please, dial the number of our attorney…" Mr. Bang was absorbed by a feeling of apathy and he felt like taking poison. "Oh, it is Saturday today… Find his home number…"

Bang had barely enough time to formulate his request as the phone on his desk rang.

"He is calling me himself… He's probably read it already, the bastard… He can sense it when it smells like more money…"

However, it was not the attorney. It was a television station calling for an interview. In a polite colorless voice, Lockhart promised to inform Mr. Bang of the invitation and call them back immediately with a reply.

As soon as the assistant put the receiver down, the phone rang again. This time it was a journalist.

"This is not right..." murmured Bang irritably. "Tell them that I am inviting everyone for a press conference. Do they want a show? They will get it... Mr. Lockhart, gather everyone tomorrow at noon."

"Yes, sir... And where would you like to meet them?"

"Here... Let them come to me. Arrange it to be done in the dinner hall. Have the staff move the table to one side and arrange for some chairs. Therefore, by tomorrow I need to find out who exactly stands behind this... Lockhart, my dear, turn everything upside down, but at least give me one version... During the last few years I have many who have grown grudge against me, thus I am completely lost in theories of who has turned out to be so bright..."

"I hear you, sir."

"And one thing more, Lockhart..."

"Yes, sir?"

"If you please, connect with the local terrorists and tell them that we will need at least fifty kilograms of explosive. When everyone is gathered for the press conference, we will blow up the hall..."

The joke raised Mr. Bangs's mood to a small degree.

"Very good, sir," answered the secretary without even the shadow of a smile, "only allow me to amend this…"

"Yes, in what way?"

"The dinner hall has only just been repaired… If it is possible, can we blow them up on the lawn?"

"But if it rains, won't it put out the fuse?" countered Mr. Bang.

"I had not considered this, sir…"

"It is nothing, my friend, nothing at all… You will learn much, if you agree to accompany me in prison."

"It would be my privilege," answered Lockhart, as he left to inquire into the instigator of the scandal.

Mr. Bang dialed the number of attorney. He did not answer immediately.

"And why haven't you called me?" said Bang in a voice ringing with scandal and righteous offence. "Only just don't pretend that you know nothing about it."

"I know, Mr. Bang," the attorney answered in an unusually cold manner. Despite the fact that he was one of the most expensive attorneys in the kingdom, he always talked very personably with Bang.

"I am not happy with your tone… I need to understand, who is behind this…

"I am afraid, sir, that there is no secret about this whatsoever…"

"Who is this person? Who is he? The rector of one of the universities?"

"Did you not see the news?"

"What, and what did they say there about it?"

"Alas…"

"Well, so who is he?"

"It is not 'he', it is 'her'. Or to be more precise, her representatives."

"A woman? "Could it be the blonde from yesterday?" flashed in the mind of Bang.

"Her Majesty…"

Out of consternation, the receiver fell from the hands of Bang.

"So, on top of everything," and here the tone of the attorney became icy, "you are charged with the public insult towards British monarchy… I do not think that I can be of any further service to you as your attorney."

"What? Are you not afraid of losing the fee?"

"Not at all… I am a loyal Briton, sir, and I cannot protect the enemy of my Queen."

Mr. Bang flung the receiver so that it cleaved into two… "Hell, these scum poke fun at royal court, as they deem it necessary themselves, but far be it for me, a stranger, to drop a playful joke about the overthrow of monarchy, whereupon they will immediately fan the flames… In this world nothing has changed. Perhaps, they could still chop off my head by order from the highest circles… It seems that the court had not interfered into politics for 300 years… I wonder how I managed to become such a royal pain in the neck! At the same time, it might be time to clear off…"

Bang raged at these contradictory feelings. Undoubtedly, what was happening was a total catastrophe, but he could not but understand, that a scandal of this scale would raise his reputation to beyond limits of the sky. Now everything would depend on how he would present himself. If to make a few careful steps, then he can only win out from the current situation. Only now it is becoming clearer with each minute that to remain in the manor, yes even in Britain as a whole, is unsafe. Scotland Yard could appear at this doorstep at any moment. Bang feverishly rushed to arrange his departure…

"Mr. Lockhart!" yelled Nicholas, already forgetting that he could summon the secretary on the intercom.

However, Lockhart was not there.

"He has run off… Even the sky would not want to serve the enemy of its Queen… And that is what's so funny! I had nothing against the British monarchy and all the more so against its majesty! All that I wanted was to clear away the obscurity and verbiage from science… To free human thought! It is just as well that I do not have a family… There is nobody for me to protect, no one to worry about … But she believed in our family happiness… Well, as for me they will chop off my head… No, it is for the best that she is not with me… But if my secretary ran out, who would organize the press conference?"

Mister Bang turned on the TV and heard his own voice: "We are going to need at least fifty kilograms of explosive. When everyone is gathered for the press conference, we will blow up the hall…"

"This is just as bad as the nightmare! Lockhart – a traitor? When did he have the time? It had just been a joke!?

The door to the office was slowly opening. "The arresting team? The counter-terrorism group?" Bang squatted and hid behind the table in case they immediately began to shoot.

Giovanni came into the room.

"You are still not offended, that I raped Mira?" he asked gaily. "And here I am forgiving you for the fact that you slaughtered me by my own kitchen knife!"

"Of course you…" choked Bang as he got out from his hiding place.

"But I did not die. Faith has resurrected me… You know, sir, I am an earnest catholic… And, by the way, I work for the intelligence service of the Vatican. It was not good of you to criticize our contemporary cosmology. It was completely laid out by the Pope… He has sent me here in order to poison you… You do remember yesterday's broth?"

Nicholas immediately woke up… How could the cook know what he had dreamt at that night? It meant that the entire proceeding was only part of a dream. Reality and illusion slammed into each other as two runaway trains ran without brakes

"I should change something in my life", he thought, having finally awakened.

ξ

After unsaddling his horse, while in a pensive mood, he began to clean its slightly sweaty back with a brush.

“Perhaps, I should just forget about this proposal. Mikhail has clearly gone out of his mind. An electronic Messiah… He has even created a new race of monster-robots. You are only fooling yourself if you think that if you concentrate overwhelming power in yourself, then you will manage it better than others have done so in the past. Power, in general, should on no account ever be concentrated into the hands of a few… Let us assume that Mikhail is right, and let us also assume that in the full course of time everything will happen exactly so, and that people will at long last finally begin to fully utilize solar energy, and artificial intelligence will actively participate in our life banishing the effects of human stupidity and unpredictability…Yet this could never happen in a single moment, not even with the help of one more revolution. With humankind it is necessary to relate to it with great care much the same as with a little child with no sense of its own.”

Mr. Bang locked up the stable and returned to the manor. The pervasive smell of the horse rose up from him and it dawned on him that he badly needed to change his clothes and take a shower. He loved the sensation of the cleanly scrubbed body, but hated the process of it, especially when once he was by himself in the manor. The water muffled noises from the outside, and to Mr. Bang it seemed that when it was absent, something unpleasant was occurring in the manor. This time he tried to keep the process to a minimum of time.

Finally refreshed, he was dressed and ready to for dinner at the Red Lion, but suddenly again the Russian girl came to his mind, the girl with whom he had so unpleasantly parted on the previous Friday.

"And what if I invite her to go with me to the restaurant?" thought Mr. Bang, and this thought was pleasing to him.

After being connected to the agency, he asked to send him the same girl.

"OK, we will connect with her and let you know if she will be free this evening," the voice on the phone was restrained - polite, as if the discussion dealt with an appointment to visit the doctor.

In about half an hour the phone rang.

"I am sorry, sir. Miss Nellie will not be able to come to you. We can send you another girl."

"But I wanted only Nellie. Is that her real name?"

On the phone he heard a discreet giggle. On the agency website, even the faces of all the girls in the photographs were blacked out. "For sure that is not her real name," thought Mr. Bang.

"Mr. Bang, you know our rules. We simply help the encounter between people, and which happens between the two if – is not our concern… Miss Nellie said that it she did not want to meet with you."

"Please tell her, that I want to apologize… And to invite her to a restaurant. And there is more. I will pay her seven hundred fifty… So a pair of hours would be the same as for the whole night!"

"OK, we will let you know."

In a few minutes the agency reported that Nellie had agreed and would arrive in about forty minutes.

"If you please, prepare the money and pay in advance… Do not make the girl wait."

Mr. Bang went into his office where, in the box which stood on the book shelf behind the statuette of the exiled Napoleon with the ball and chain riveted to his foot, he stored a thousand pounds for unforeseen expenditures. Apparently, the fact that Napoleon was chained up, suggested that Mr. Bang had trust in this single-minded conqueror of Europe.

"He was also a peacemaker…" he muttered acidly, counting out the necessary sum and affectionately flicking the statuette of Napoleon on the nose.

This time Nellie seemed to Mr. Bang to be even younger and more attractive that the "original" picture, he had carried in its head.

"How do you do, Nellie!" he said in Russian, and without delay handed the girl the bundle of pink fifty pound bank notes with the solemn portraits of the Queen. "If Her Majesty only knew what I am paying for with her image", flashed in his head.

"How do you do, sir", the girl said as she counted the money and stashed it into her bag. She efficiently began to undo her blouse, but Mr. Bang stopped her.

"First of all, I wanted to apologize for my behavior last Friday…"

"Not at all, it was nothing sir. I, honestly speaking, was not offended. It was innocent enough and it is not an issue. You did not try to rape me with a beer bottle."

"God forbid… But did you not want to meet me earlier? Didn't that mean that I did offend you after all?"

"I was just busy… I am a student at the university."

"In Cambridge? What are you studying?"

"I am earning an academic degree in scientific prostitution," Nellie joked with a serious face. "Tomorrow is Monday. We have an examination on safe sex."

"No, seriously?"

"I am studying medicine. To be more precise - neurosurgery."

"Listen to me, Nellie, I want to invite you for a walk. The weather seems to be outstanding, and then after that we can have dinner."

"But then we would not have time for any sex… I only have two hours."

"In that case we can keep it to a walk and supper."

"I am flattered… Well then, as you wish."

They left the manor and passed by the church.

"It is beautiful around here…" Nellie noted in an affable manner. Now her behavior differed in no way from the behavior of any other girl, and it seemed that she was in no way involved in such exotic types of employment.

"And so, since I have just gotten seven hundred fifty pounds from you, I feel myself obliged to somehow entertain you…"

"Tell me about yourself…"

"Am I really that interesting to you? Well then, as you wish. My parents are in Russia. They are well-off people. They sent me to study at Cambridge. And that is my entire story."

"But then, what made you get into this?"

"What?" Nellie asked innocently and began to laugh in a silvery tone.

"Neurosurgery…" Mr. Bang supported her joke.

"I suffer from an extreme form of feminism, and also an insatiable sexual need… So that contact with men in this particular context – is my hobby."

"What an interesting admission from the mouth of such a young girl… How old are you?"

"Oh, that is such a tactless question…"

"Excuse me…"

"Well then. I am twenty two, since you've already asked…"

"I could be your father…"

"What a very proper observation."

"To me it seemed that you were older," sighed Mr. Bang with obvious regret.

"So why you did you pry after my age? Indeed it seems that it is necessary to be careful that your call girl does not end up being younger than is required … There could be trouble. Although I consider that by this the bigotry of our times is surely manifested."

"I wanted to propose heart and soul to you," Bang suddenly joked, "but you are younger than me by eighteen years…"

She giggled.

"So you have decided to be married to a prostitute?"

"To a neurosurgeon."

"Are you serious?"

"It is more than that. I wanted to propose heart and soul to you."

"Why a neurosurgeon? Is everything all right with you in your head?"

"I have wanted for a long time now to understand what I actually do have inside my head…"

"Believe me, it is not a very pretty picture…"

"Once upon a time, in my long gone youth, I worked as a medical orderly in the morgue, so you cannot shock me… I also saw a lot."

"This is pretty nice … a shocking convergence of interests. However, in any event it would be necessary for me to say no to you."

"Why?"

"I am not ready to get married."

"At all?"

"It's just not for me. I do not believe in the institution of marriage."

They went on for some time in silence. The girl increasingly pleased Mr. Bang. She, in some magical manner, reminded him of Mira

"Well, can I at least propose being friends to you?"

"I am afraid we can only do this within the framework of our of price list. I am sorry."

"It's nothing, nothing… That is completely logical."

The supper began in a dull manner. Mr. Bang kept silent. Nellie, however, was not bored and she told him without any hesitation about her dreams. For example, she had recently dreamed that she was a dragon that would belch out flames. Mr. Bang noted that the dreams of the dragon foreboded good luck and must necessarily be about something that was desired or wished for that the dragon could grant. In response to that Nellie logically noted that when you dreamt about yourself being the dragon that it was completely unclear to whom you could make such a request. After that Mr. Bang treated his companion to the legend of his manor; and Nellie noted that she pitied the unhappy nun, but that she felt no pity at all for the monk, since all of the resulting grief was definitely his fault.

"She trusted herself to him, and he…"

"And he what?"

"And he destroyed her. If you are going to please a girl, you must ensure her safety. You should organize a normal departure, but not jump over hurdles… Your monk definitely ruined the girl for nothing… "

Bang sighed heavily. He thought, what if he told her about his history with Mira, she would then unconditionally accuse him of doing everything just like the unhappy monk from the legend. And then he would try to explain that there were different circumstances…

He called for a cab. In a stressful silence, both keeping their thoughts to themselves, they finally arrived at the manor; they said goodbye to each other in a matter of fact manner, and the cab drove away with his might – have – been spouse on the way to New Market, where the road turned towards Cambridge.

Mr. Bang grudgingly kindled the fireplace, which seemed to not want to give off any heat, and after smoking cigar, arranged himself next to the fire and started to converse with himself in an irritated manner.

"And now we have it that a prostitute has turned me down… Even she did not want to marry me. No one wants to share their life with me. Should I buy a dog, at least, as the classic author advised? It's too bad, that I hate dogs. If life lasted only for a short holiday of one-and-a-half hours, everyone would muster all their strength and live it worthily. But instead it is one long trial, and however much you persevere and carry on, sooner or later you will be turned into a court fool who has lost his mind… It is all a farce, and nothing but a farce.

Mr. Bang sat somewhat dully looking at the fire, and then he threw the butt end of the cigar into the fireplace and went to his office, where it started to check his electronic mail. Almost immediately his eyes fell upon a letter from a reader.

Dear Mr. Bang!

As it happens I read your book by coincidence. Mr. Bang, may I tell you what I think? I will speak honestly, and this might be hard for you. But on no account do I want to be rude. And I would not want to offend you in any way. And therefore I will not do that. Mr. Bang, this is all nonsense! All of your philosophizings is not worth a hill of beans. This is because there is no truth or essence in any of them. First of all, either you really do not understand (which is highly improbable), or else you are subconsiously hiding the facts (which is more likely). All people behave in accordance with some motivation. And I mean that one should examine the motives of human behavior as a philosopher! Motives depend on a huge number of factors. But this is – a longer discussion. It is possible to make an easier comparison. Higher mathematics is a very complex science. But the essence of it is based on elementary arithmetic, i.e., on four operations. But they are in their turn only part of the same set of operations, - addition and subtraction (multiplication - this the same as addition, but only by several times, and division is the reverse process of that). The basing of the most complex mathematics on the simplest arithmetic is not denied by even the professionals. In exactly the same manner, the entirety of computer technology is based on - only one type of operation - 0 or 1. Or in other words - there is or there is not; on or off.. To add or to take away. Plus or minus. There it is, the essence of things. Even the most extremely complicated things available for one's examination can turn out to be simple.

But I have not seen this from you as a "philosopher". You cannot even point to a motivation for your behavior, yet you deign to discuss those of others. And, you were born in Russia; yet, you live in Great Britain. In between the two you lived somewhere else (Finland). What was the motivation for your behavior then? I think that in essence you are of the same species of Homo

Sapiens as that of any bum on the street. And whatever else may be said about the inhumanity of Hitler, he was also a member of Homo Sapiens. He certainly wasn't a dog or a crocodile. And his comrades still recall every now and then his all too humane traits. We also know that in his youth he drew, and it was pretty good. But whom did he become, how so, and why did he become such an icon? And most of all, how could this quite inhumane creature suddenly induce millions of completely respectable and law-abiding Germans follow him? That would be something about which it would be worthwhile to ponder for a philosopher, and not to prattle on about this other nonsense. One doesn't need to hear about historical convulsions from philosophy. Philosophy also exists in private life, such as in the relations between a husband and a wife. Philosophy is the science of sciences. For you, however, it seems like this is more of a hobby. It is just a play on words, from which there is no true sense of things or events.

With best wishes to you.

Again, it is far from my wish to give you any insult, and I simply wanted to openly and honestly express my point of view to you.

C.

Mr. Bang suddenly placed his hands in front of himself on the table, buried his head in his hands and began to sob. It wasn't so much that he wasn't used to getting contrary opinions. But for today this was the last drop. Philosophy which was the main point of his life was just all nonsense. He himself was just such shit, that even a prostitute had rejected his offer of marriage. A passing fancy crossed his mind, one of suicide…

Somewhere within the deepest well of his sorrow, Mr. Bang began to be overcome with a feeling of calm. He could see himself as if from the outside; with a pattern of clear thought and awareness, that this was simply a series of nervous disruptions, and that it was definitely better that this was happening now when no one else could see him in such a condition.

"I can't even cry like a normal human being," he finally growled. "These thoughts are always climbing into the head. I hate it! I hate my cursed rational way of thought!" His sobs subsided, in a vague feeling of relief, as if he'd pissed away his worries. Life is so huge and intractable, that no one can ever really grasp it all, either stretching or cutting off one's appendages as one goes through daily life – just as the Bed of Polypemon, that robber of Greek myth whose bed would fit anyone, and it would – after he either stretched or cut off their legs to make the fit work out in the end. It always spews out its tasty scandals, the tragicomic scenes in parallel with bullshit, with its innumerable treasures of vulgarities, to the exaltation of the sources of idiocy. Oh My God, I am so tired! Lord, forgive me, Lord! Nothing is helping at all. Not the mountain of the books nor heap of money… I do not have anything at all… What is the good of all this? Why?"

And then, out of the blue Mr. Bang calmed down and straightened up. He became somewhat easier and light headed. Out of the corner of his eye, he spied a beetle that was trying to crawl up out of a bin of papers, but each time it got a certain distance it would lose traction and roll back downwards. Nicholas carefully tilted the bin, and the beetle was successfully released to its liberty.

"Could it be possible that this simple action was the whole point of my life? It was to save this poor bug from starving to death?"

Monday began in a restless fashion. Several times the telephone rang. Mr. Bang woke up in a disgusted state of mind and had to force himself not to open his mail before breakfast just in order not to lose his appetite in the end. And for that same reason he testily kept himself away from the morning newspapers.

Giovanni was unusually sullen and did not say anything at all about the adventures of the previous weekend. He only politely inquired:

"Will your friend not be joining us for dinner, sir?"

"No, he has gone already."

Mr. Lockhart raised an eyebrow in an inquiring manner but asked nothing out loud. He thought to himself that if it became necessary to then he would include it in the business appointments of Mr. Bang, and if the meeting had no relation to business, the there was no need for him to put any further thought into the matter.

After breakfast the secretary began to reconcile the accounts, and Mr. Bang sat himself at the computer. He usually checked out various reports, sent from the numerous centers, and then would finally decide at the last moment to calibrate the course of his stocks for the day.

At first he did not believe his eyes. The numbers seemed all wrong.

"What the hell!" cursed Mr. Bang.

"Can I help you, sir?" answered secretary lightly

"If we are to believe what this idiotic screen is showing, then I have lost about three million pounds!"

"It is possible, sir, that this is connected with the general downward dip in the exchange. Have you not heard the news?"

"No… Why have not reported this to me?"

> "Sir, you did not request me to report on the status of the stock exchange. Usually you follow the stock prices yourself. If you wish it, I would be happy to examine the quotes every morning…"

"Ah. Drop it, leave it at that…Business as usual. Keep going over the accounts…"

Mr. Bang's assets were estimated to be approximately one hundred thirty million pounds sterling. Certainly the loss of three millions could not possibly ruin it. But what if that was only the beginning of something? In one way or another Mr. Bang entered into a heightened sense of awareness whenever it was necessary to make important decisions. His first notion was to sell off a large portion of the stock and wait it out until the stock market had settled.

"No, that would be stupid. On no account will I sell a single share of stock," he thought. "I will wait still several days until the situation has stabilized."

Mr. Bang plunged his head deep into an analysis of the news around the world. For him it was necessary to understand what exactly had caused the fluctuations on the stock market. The impression emerged that there was no single factor behind what was happening. In any case, the foundations of the question were not involved with the crisis in the oil market. Quite simply, the general economic situation had deteriorated, pulling down all the stock prices, including those which belonged to Mr. Bang.

Just in case it were otherwise, he consulted with his broker, but that person also confirmed that he thought that the dip in the market was temporary and no drastic actions were really needed. Mr. Bang, however, could not relax and checked any interesting movements in the market for the entire day.

On that day, the design for the cover jacket of his new book "The Philosophy of the Future", arrived for his approval; but even this did not distract him from the steadfastly monotonous tracking of the stock exchange.

On the next day his position deteriorated further. The losses of Mr. Bang now amounted to more than six million pounds sterling. He could wait no longer. On Wednesday Mr. Bang issued on order to sell the greater part of his stock holdings, and to transfer any proceeds from the sales into his current accounts at Barclays Bank.

Mr. Bang could obtain five percent bank interest from this sum, which after the payment of taxes came to two hundred seventy thousand pounds per month, or, simply stated, sixty seven thousand pounds per week. Such money would provide Mr. Bang with sufficient means to exercise practically any fantasies and entertainments he wished, while keeping with the fact that his principal would remain untouched. Certainly, in Britain, a certain percentage of inflation was observed and the retention of capital would be illusory. However, if Mr. Bang were able to spend only that part of the percentage which was given to him that was over the inflation rate, then his main capital would actually remain untouched.

But Mr. Bang had some fairly hefty financial commitments. Up to this point he had financed the work of several research centers; he was involved with charity work; and these activities, as a matter of course, ate away at his capital. And the rate at which Mr. Bang had allowed himself for contributions to charity currently ran to more than one hundred twenty thousand pounds per month. However, no one had ever said that Mr. Bang had to keep supporting all of these undertakings. So, with a single stroke of his pen, or better yet, with the uttering of a simple phrase, and by such a simple action would thus impel an order via Mr. Lockhart, and then – a couple dozen scientists who had been feeding off of Mr. Bang's largesse would soon find themselves on the street, and the centers would be closed.

An entire village in Sudan could thrive and flourish, on account of the efforts to provide support dispensed by Mr. Bang amounting to nothing more than a mere eight thousand pounds per month, - and that in accord with his financial position, who would not have any impact on it at all. Nevertheless, the scientists would have found themselves a new cow to milk…

"And so what's wrong if I do that?" Mr. Bang amused himself with the fantasy. "At the moment all of my activities are considered to be a joke, so then no one needs them … Well, let them all go to hell. At least I have covered myself, thank God, to the end of my… I am surrounded by the quiet hatred of my allies and by the open hatred of my enemies. Why do I need any of this?"

And in reflecting thus, Mr. Bang gently fooled himself: he knew it was hardly likely he could do such a thing. Well perhaps it was possible for him to consider, without further ceremony, just exactly what he thought he was going to do with his life, and what he would achieve in this life? Mr. Bang was still only forty years old, and a complete picture of health. But how would he occupy himself with the remaining thirty or forty years of his life? Because, if he was bored even with such an active and dynamic life, what would be there to say about it when inevitably there was an absence of activity and dynamism?

Mr. Bang wanted to flee from the heat and bustle of the manor. In the office the cleaning lady was moving about, and the cook was making a fuss about something in the kitchen. He was actually preparing to cook a Peking Duck and was discussing it in a lively manner with the housekeeper, going on about how he would hang the duck in a certain way in the oven so that it would not be cooked in its own juices.

"Mr. Lockhart, call the chauffer. I would like to look in on Cambridge."

Mr. Bang had three automobiles, but he did not like to drive himself anywhere. The cook used the Citroen. The minibus was used for the transport of the guests of Mr. Bang: in it there were places for seven passengers as well as four television sets. For himself, Mr. Bang preferred to use the third motor vehicle, which was a luxurious Saab.

When he passed by the kitchen, he boomed out to the cook.

"Well, Giovanni, don't you want to brag to me about how it was possible for you to hang the duck up properly in the oven?"

"Sir, how did you know about that?"

"The duck sent me a letter of complaint via email regarding your lack of humanity, well, to be more precise, your lack of fatty juices, in dealing with it."

Ah, then you must have heard my conversation with Sandra..." surmised the cook. "I wanted to do it just so that they would come out juicy, and that the skin would be crackling."

Mr. Bang glanced into the oven. There quite efficiently were hung two ducks, strung up by the wings between the racks, and set in the upper part of the oven.

"By way of explanation, sir, the place where I buy the ducks, sells them without the necks. But, the Chinese hang the ducks up by the neck. I specially looked up the recipe and even saw a program on TV."

"Giovanni, you are a genius."

"Well, it's nothing. But were you not telling me about the cover jacket for your new book? So because of that I couldn't control myself and decided to share with you this discovery…"

"Don't rush it… they might suddenly just fall when they start to heat up…"

"I've tied them with a special cord…"

"In Russia, when they wanted to get the same effect, they fried chicken in a bottle…"

"But wouldn't this be considered a desecration of the bird?"

Mr. Bang called to his mind the phrase about the beer bottle that was made by Nellie, and suddenly he was disgusted with himself.

"Well, it's quite OK, Giovanni. I have to go now."

"But you should try some when it is hot!" the cook quickly took out a casserole dish and began to lay out pieces of meat into the dish. "I cannot let you go out without having eaten!"

"I will return by dinner… I do not want to eat now…"

However, excuses were useless. Mr. Bang tried the roasted meat. But, the meat was a bit hard to chew.

"Is it too firm?" asked the cook cautiously.

"It is quite good, but it could probably use a little more cooking…"But why are you serving us this roasted feast today, this duck?"

"So that you would not go any more to this outrageous, gross "Red Lion". Eat at home today!"

"You are my mother. More than that, you're my Italian mother… Nicholas began to laugh.

Chauffeur was detained for a little bit, and Mr. Bang thought, why not sit down and drive by himself? But, then at that moment, the Saab came up the driveway, and he climbed into the rear seat and sat himself.

"Let's go into Cambridge by the Newmarket Road, for nice easy drive," he said and he sunk deep into his thoughts.

"So that's how it is… For the cook, his concerns are simple and plain, but for him they represent his entire point in life. How to hang the duck up in the oven, to make it crispier or not… To throw all he's got into it and to devote entire days to the consideration of the finer points of various culinary recipes… But that is an illusion. If we do not run forward strongly enough, then it will turn out that there are forces behind us that will force us to move. And why did I leave for the city? It was just impossible for me to stay at home. My office - such refinements, such luxuries, have now became for me the camera of tortures. These several days gone by, until the drop in the stock market, seem to have cost me three years of life. How is that! In three days I have lost an entire amount that possibly another person would not even make in his entire life!"

At the entrance to Cambridge the car stopped at a traffic signal. There, right in front of Mr. Bang's eyes appeared a billboard of a tourist agency.

"Go to Saint Petersburg!" he whispered and then, with saying anything to the chauffeur, he left the car.

ISBN 978-1-105-68739-6
90000
9 781105 687396

www.ingramcontent.com/pod-product-compliance
Ingram Content Group UK Ltd.
Pitfield, Milton Keynes, MK11 3LW, UK
UKHW040602210726
13854UKWH00008B/1757

9 781105 687396